C000127454

Praise for

Johnnie and Will
CURSE OF THE DEVIL'S SON

Johnnie and his mum, trapped in a life with a miserable benefactor, turn to a 200-year-old ghost pirate and create a new life on his ship. Captain Will is cursed by The Devil's Son in a way that only allows souls as miserable as he to see him. Can Johnnie, Laura and Will find a way to help each other? Can the curse be lifted and the pirate set free?

On an island off the coast of Florida, Johnnie finds himself without friends, without a father to stand by him and without much hope that his mother will ever be happy again. Wandering in exploration, he finds an old rundown ship in the harbour, and in the galley below, the captain himself...the cursed soul of Captain Will.

Johnnie's mum, Laura, having married the miserable Nathaniel as a means to escape poverty in England, concocts a plan to save Johnnie from being grounded forever. It turns out that her plan can save them all. The old ship is brought back to life, and eventually a new life is formed and an old life is brought to peace.

Every kid loves a good ghost story and adding pirates to the mix is always a good idea. Stevie Smith has begun a writing career that will undoubtedly touch the lives of many children. What better pirate treasure is there than that which can spark the imagination of a child? What better gift to the world than a story that proves that good overcomes evil? No curse is strong enough to conquer love. This author shows promise, and "Johnnie and Will" promises to be a good read.

—Heather Froeschl, Quilldipper

More praise for

Johnnie and Will
CURSE OF THE DEVIL'S SON

Johnnie is an average kid living in England. He loves his family and has a great life, but his life gets flip turned upside down when his dad mysteriously disappears. He lived alone with his mother until the house was taken from them. They have nowhere to go, but Johnnie's mum marries a horrible man named Nathaniel and they move to America. When Johnnie is out wandering around a dock he stumbles upon an old pirate.... The adventure follows....

I thought that this was a brilliant story, very original, with a strong backbone. I couldn't put it down and loved every minute of it. I turned each page with anticipation of what dramatic event would take place next. The book is extraordinarily well written and made me picture every moment. As Johnnie delved into more danger and conspiracy, I really felt myself living it with him. I only hope there are many more books by Stevie Smith, as I thoroughly enjoyed this one and look forward to reading more."

—Tom Graham, who plays Robert in BBC One's *Byker Grove.*

Johnnie and Will
CURSE OF THE DEVIL'S SON

by

Stevie Smith

PublishAmerica
Baltimore

© 2004 by Stevie Smith.
All rights reserved. No part of this book may be reproduced, stored in a retrieval system or transmitted in any form or by any means without the prior written permission of the publishers, except by a reviewer who may quote brief passages in a review to be printed in a newspaper, magazine or journal.

First printing

ISBN: 1-4137-2322-5
PUBLISHED BY PUBLISHAMERICA, LLLP
www.publishamerica.com
Baltimore

Printed in the United States of America

Dedications

To Anne—Words are not enough.
To my family and friends for all their support—
Too many to mention but they know who they are—

Thank You

Acknowledgements

James Erskine Photography, Dunfermline.

CONTENTS

CHAPTER ONE
The Curse

They had arrived on Pearl Bay Island two weeks ago but already Johnnie was bored. Maybe things would be different when school reopened after the summer holidays, but in the meantime he didn't know a soul. He missed London, and his friends. He resented his mother and Nathaniel for making him move to Florida. The house was nice enough and there was a big piece of land around it that would have been great for football if he had anybody here to play with.

Nathaniel and Laura had busied themselves about the house since they arrived. They rarely spoke to each other, or to Johnnie. In the evenings after dinner Nathaniel would read while Laura watched the television with the sound turned down very low as if she were afraid of disturbing him. Johnnie would often catch his mother staring out of the window into space, but when he asked if there was anything wrong, she never answered. She would just shake her head. He knew that she was sad but he couldn't understand why she was taking it out on him. It seemed like a very long time since she had held him or said something nice to him. He was fed up hanging around the house but when he complained about being bored Nathaniel had simply growled and told him to stop whining and go and amuse himself out in the yard.

"Children nowadays just don't know how to play anymore. When I was young we didn't…" and he was off, muttering to himself as usual.

Johnnie opened the back door and sat in the yard alone, remembering happier times and wishing he were back in London, until Laura called him in for bed.

"I hope tomorrow is as much fun as today," he muttered to her as he went upstairs.

That was what his old teacher used to call sarcasm.

The next morning Johnnie had just finished washing, and brushing his teeth when he heard a knock on the door. Nathaniel came in and said, "Clean this room up, boy. It's like a pigsty. After breakfast there's chores to be done. You're to tidy up the weeds in the garden. Then you can go and explore the island."

Johnnie hated working in the garden, but to keep Nathaniel from scowling he would work hard. Then he would be free to see what the island was all about, and with any luck meet some new friends.

Johnnie weeded, dug the earth and bagged all the rubbish. He stood up to stretch his aching legs. His back felt like it was breaking and blisters were forming on his hands from using the shovel. He heard Nathaniel open the door and shout, "That will do, I suppose. Be back for dinner, and don't be late. We ain't cooking a meal so it can go to waste on your account, boy."

Johnnie wished that someone could have said, "Well done. You've made a difference."

Maybe one day my mum will be proud of me or even like me again. No use moping around; there's an island to discover.

The sun felt warm on his back as he set off to see if anybody was fishing or if there were any kids swimming. It should be easy to find the water. Nathaniel had said that every road in Pearl Bay ended at the water's edge. After jogging for about ten minutes he spotted a sign for the harbour. *There will be people coming and going there and maybe some other kids to talk to.*

The harbour was small with only a few boats, but one boat was different from the rest. It was really old and damaged, the masts were broken and there were no sails. As Johnnie moved closer, the boat seemed to get bigger and more mysterious looking.

"Hello, anybody there?" Johnnie shouted.

No answer.

"Hello, anybody there?"

Nothing.

Maybe the boat didn't belong to anyone. It was rotten and damaged. No harm in going on board to take a look. But the boat had drifted from the pier. Johnnie stepped back, took a long run up and launched himself onto the deck of the boat. He picked himself up and looked around. There were so many holes everywhere; he was surprised the boat hadn't sunk. It must have been beautiful when it was new. Maybe it was a pirate ship with real pirates sailing around the world, stealing from other boats and ships. It could have been Blackbeard's or the ship Long John Silver had sailed.

There might be some clues below. He climbed down the stairs slowly to avoid the rotten steps. He strained to see. It was so dark and creaky; he was feeling uneasy.

Maybe this wasn't such a good idea...It's only an old boat. Be brave.

Suddenly a voice from the dark boomed, "What are you doing 'ere?"

The voice sent shivers from his spine to the tips of his toes. He tripped down the last step and fell onto his hands and knees. His head was spinning and his throat had closed up.

"I'll ask you one more time," roared the voice, "and if you don't answer me, I'll feed you to the sharks."

Johnnie's mouth was dry and he was shaking with fear but he knew he had to answer the voice. He'd seen the film *Jaws* and didn't fancy being shark-feed.

"I'm s-sorry mister, for b-being on your b-boat. I only w-wanted to have a look around," Johnnie stuttered, trembling.

"You 'ave no right to be snooping around here. Were you thinking of stealing from me, boy?" snarled the voice.

"N-no mister, honest, I just w-wanted to see if this was a p-pirate boat," Johnnie stuttered.

"Boat? This is a ship, boy. Pirates sail in ships. And a mighty fine ship she was, too, in her day," boomed the voice. "What's your name, boy? I've not seen you around these parts before."

"M-my name is Johnnie and I've just moved here from England with my mum and stepdad," he answered, still trembling.

In the gloom, Johnnie could just make out the figure of a man sitting at an old table. Fearing the worst, he wondered what the man would do to him.

"Come over here, boy, and sit down," said the voice gruffly.

Slowly, Johnnie walked over to the table. He was petrified and could feel beads of sweat dripping down his neck. It was too gloomy to see much, but creepy visions were going through his head as he tried to put a face to the voice.

"Hurry up, boy, I haven't got all day," growled the voice.

Moving quickly, he fumbled his way into an old wooden chair and looked across the table into the face of the man who was sitting there. His hair was as black as coal and tied back in a ponytail. His eyes were as blue as the ocean but terribly sad looking. For some reason Johnnie didn't feel frightened any more.

"How do you like my ship, boy?" the man quizzed.

"Awesome!" said Johnnie.

The man smiled and said proudly, "She was the queen of the sea in her day, boy. No finer pirate ship sailed the seven seas."

"I knew it! I just knew it was a pirate ship," Johnnie said, bursting with excitement. "Are you a real pirate, like Blackbeard?"

The pirate's face twisted into a snarl.

"He weren't a pirate, boy. He were a vicious dog, with no honour, I told him that 'n' all. I wouldn't have spat on him if he were on fire. He only cared about himself, and couldn't give a damn about his crew, or anyone else for that matter. He would beat his men like dogs if they didn't fall into line. He were a disgrace to the pirate code, so he were, lad. He ruled by fear because that was the only way he could get respect," he said.

There was a long uncomfortable silence, and then the pirate slumped forward and covered his face with his huge, trembling hands.

"It should have been that dog that met my fate. Damn this curse! Damn it, damn it, damn it!"

"Curse? What curse?" asked Johnnie, quietly.

The pirate slowly lifted his head from his hands and Johnnie could tell that he had been crying.

"I didn't mean to upset you by talking about Blackbeard; I'm really, really sorry," said Johnnie, feeling sorry for the pirate.

There was another eerie silence and then, with his voice trembling, the pirate said, "He were the least of my worries, boy."

Johnnie was annoyed with himself for making the pirate so sad. *It seems that annoying people and making them sad is all I'm good at.*

"You look like a smart lad to me," said the pirate. "So I'm going to ask you a question. Now think about it, lad. How many years ago did Blackbeard sail the seven seas?"

Johnnie thought for a second or two then answered, "About two hundred, I suppose."

The pirate watched the look of fear creep back into Johnnie's eyes.

"N-no! You're a g-ghost!" he gasped.

Johnnie stood up and slowly started edging his way back towards the stairs.

"Now, now, lad, don't be panickin'. I'm not gonna hurt you. Come on, sit down," said the pirate softly.

Trembling with fear, Johnnie sat and they stared at each other across the table for what seemed like an eternity. When the silence was broken the pirate's voice was as soft and as smooth as silk. "Two lifetimes ago, lad, I used to be the captain of this here pirate ship. Her name was *The Morada*. I sailed all over the seven seas in her, to distant countries, capturing ships and boats that were delivering fancy clothes and gold to kings, queens, sultans and the like. We would steal all manner of strange and wonderful things and sell them in all sorts of exotic, far away places. We never fired our cannons on anybody that didn't fire on us first and we never hurt anyone for the sake of it. When we captured a ship we'd tie the crew up and take the bounty but we always left them with something of value 'cause we knew the crews were sailing the seas to feed the mouths of their women and young uns. Then we'd be on our way. You had to be on your toes though, lad, because at any moment, other pirates could come out of the mist, take yer spoils, and leave you with nothing.

"Then of course there were the king's lawmen to worry about. They would put you on the gallows if they caught you with stolen bounty. They would chase us hard, tryin' to catch us with bounty on board, but they could never capture *The Morada*. You see, lad, my ship was as fast as the wind and my crew were the best ever to sail the seven seas."

The pirate lowered his head, paused for a moment, sighed, and continued, "We'd heard that a Spanish galleon, laden with gold sovereigns and precious jewels, was sailing the seas, so we decided to set out and capture it. If all we'd heard was true, we could give up the pirate's life, go home to our families and live like kings. We were no time at all at sea when a storm blew in. The waves were as big as mountains and the winds were mighty strong so I gave the crew the order to head back to shore, rather than risk lives."

The pirate stopped speaking, clenched his fists and laid both arms on the table, his whole body shaking.

"Are you okay?" asked Johnnie, still frightened, but intrigued.

The pirate continued to speak, but his voice was even softer, "We were not far from home, when we were taken by surprise. I should 'ave 'ad me wits about me, but the winds were throwing and battering *The Morada* like a cork in a pond. Suddenly, from out of the wind, rain and darkness, came *The Spawn,* a ship that I thought was only real in the minds of drunken old sailors. The howling and shrieking that came from her would have curdled your blood, lad. We were so close to home that we just weren't expecting to be boarded. We tried to fight them off, but my men were outnumbered."

The pirate looked up to the ceiling, placed both hands behind his head, closed his eyes, and as he continued, tears fell down his rugged face.

"They took the ship in no time at all, bound all my crew, held a dagger to my throat and tied me to the mast. The howling and shrieking stopped and there was an eerie silence as the crew of *The Spawn* fell to their knees and raised their hands above their heads. Then, from out of the blackness appeared The Devil's Son, the embodiment of a hundred old men's tales. A more evil-looking sight, I have never seen. He had a scar from ear to ear, teeth like small black daggers, and his bald head bore a tattoo of a skull and cross bones. His eyes had the kind of cold hard look that could make grown men quake with fear. I had heard many a yarn about his evil ways and how the Devil and his henchmen had built *The Spawn* in the bowels of hell. I 'ave never been so frightened or so sure that we were all about to die.

"I had heard tell that whenever he captured a ship, he would kill all on board but one poor soul. 'Go back amongst men and tell them you have met The Devil's Son,' he would say to this poor wretch as he stood quaking with fear. I stood awaiting my own fate, praying that God would have mercy on all of our souls. The Devil's Son and his crew ripped *The Morada* apart but found nothing.

"'Where?' he said to me, smiling in a way that sent ice through my veins.

'We've no bounty. The winds were agin us.' I says to him. He grabbed the rigging and began to swing to and fro' across the ship, squealing and laughing. 'The winds were agin us, the winds were agin us,' he squealed, in frenzy.

"Laughing hysterically, he swung for what seemed like an eternity, looking up to the sky, squealing again and again, 'The winds were agin us. The winds were agin us.'

"Then, with my own eyes, I witnessed the evil I'd heard tell of in old men's yarns, come to life. The Devil's Son jumped off the rigging and landed next to me. 'Wrong answer, my friend,' he said, smiling at me. He took out his cutlass and, staring at me all the while, he very slowly ran it through each of my men. One at a time I heard their screams and watched as the blood ran from their terrified bodies. I will never forget the pain and fear etched in their faces, or the delight in the faces of The Devil's Son and his crew as the deck turned crimson. 'In the name of God. No!' I screamed, but this only made him laugh and sing louder. He was soaked in my crew's blood as he walked towards me, smirking.

"'What kind of beast are you?' I roared. He just smiled at me and squealed, 'The wind was agin us! The wind was agin us!' The closer he came, the louder he squealed. 'The wind was agin us, the wind was agin us!'

"I summoned what strength I had left and screamed at him, 'Beast!' Then, with all the venom I could summon, I spat in the face of The Devil's Son. 'You'd better run me through 'n' all, because I won't rest until I've made you pay for this,' I roared. The squealing stopped but still he kept smiling. 'I think something special is in order, for you friend,' he said.

"His crew fell to their knees as he walked to the middle of the ship. He raised his hands to the heavens, thrashed his head forward and roared, 'Eternal Father of Darkness come to thine own.'

"I swear, lad, the blackest clouds I 'ave ever seen gathered and lightning ripped through the sky, like a cutlass through flesh. The Devil's Son then did the Devil's work. He said to me, 'You, my friend, will walk alone through the living, visible only to souls as tormented as your own. Then, only when you find woman-love, will you be released from this curse by death,' and he screamed with delight.

"His men rampaged through *The Morada,* smashing and destroying everything in their path. 'Fine crew, they bled well!' said The Devil's Son, as he swung onto *The Spawn.* They sailed off into the darkness, but I could still hear the blood-curdling shrieking and laughing as they disappeared into the night.

"At sunrise, a ship came alongside, and Captain Charles Maddock and five of his crew boarded *The Morada.* Maddock was the King's lawman, a decent man I'd been outwitting for years. He knew I was a pirate, but could never catch me with any bounty. Maddock would come into the inn and say, 'One day, Mr. Francis, one day.'

As Maddock came closer, I dropped to my knees sobbing, 'Captain, thank God.'

Maddock stood and stared at my blood-soaked crew, his face as grey as stone. 'In God's name, what animals would be capable of such a thing?' he said, his voice trembling.

'It was the work of The Devil's Son,' I screamed. I could see that Maddock was sick to his stomach, but he said, 'Wrap the bodies, weigh them down, and we will bury them at sea. Francis was a decent fellow. God will have mercy on his soul.'

"'Captain, I'm not dead, I'm right here in front of you!' I screamed, finally realising that he could neither see nor hear me. I could only watch as they prayed for our souls and then lowered the bodies one by one into the sea. 'Wash down the ship, rope her up and we'll tow her back to Pearl Bay.'

"It was then that Maddock turned to one of his men and sighed, 'I'm not looking forward to informing Mrs. Francis and the children of this.' May God forgive me, but with all that had happened I'd not thought of my wife and family. What would become of them? I'd never be able to hold my wife or girls again. I truly was cursed. They towed *The Morada* back home, tied her up, and I watched from afar as Captain Maddock informed my wife and girls of my death. I can still see them huddled together screaming, 'No! No!' From that day, I 'ave never left *The Morada*. I would not give The Devil's Son the satisfaction of seeing me watch as my wife, my children and their children's children passed over to the other side."

The pirate then leaned back and stared upwards. His eyes were filled with tears, which streamed down his face. Johnnie's mouth was dry and he had a huge lump in his throat. He was sure that if he started to cry he would never stop. All of a sudden the pirate wiped his eyes and said, "Anyway, lad, that is all there is to know about Captain William Joseph Francis, or Captain Will as me friends used to call me."

He looked at Johnnie and smiled softly, wondering, W*hat in the world is making this young un so sad that he can see an old cursed wretch such as meself?*

"Tell me lad, how is it you can see old Will? The curse allows only those who've been as tormented as I to see me. Tell me how this can be so," said the pirate.

Johnnie lowered his head and began to speak. "Everything was fine until Dad left. One minute he was there, then he was gone. That was four years ago. I was only six so I can't remember much about what happened, but I can remember that Mum and Dad never argued. So why would he leave? My friend's parents argue all the time but they're still together. I used to get up early on the morning of every birthday to wait for the postman, hoping for a card from Dad, but none ever appeared. Christmas was the same. I would meet the postman every morning as Christmas Day approached but it was the same old story, no card from Dad. Once I asked Mum why Dad had left, but she got angry and told me she didn't want to talk about it. I reckon she must have done something really bad to him and that's why she doesn't want to tell me.

"When my dad was around we used to go to lots of parties and our house was always full of people. My mum was always laughing and joking and she used to mimic people on the television. She used to swing me around by the arms till I got a tickly feeling in my tummy. I pretended that I didn't like it but I loved every minute of it. But everything changed when Dad left. Mum hardly speaks to me anymore. At least when I was at school I had my friends to talk to. We would get into trouble sometimes, but my teacher was cool and always had time for me. I hated the school holidays because I had to fend for myself. My mum worked long hours, so when she came home she would fall asleep in front of the television, wake up and go to bed. Even though she was in the house I always felt on my own.

"But this is the worst year ever. Mum has married a fat, bald, ugly American

18

man she has only just met. He treats her like dirt and hates me. He's always complaining about my manners and saying that I need to be taken in hand. He's a fat boring 'know it all' and I hate him. And now I've been dragged to this stupid place and have no friends or anybody to talk to. Why did she do this to me? Why did she have to marry someone who is horrible to us? I just want things to be how they used to be."

Johnnie covered his face with his hands and started to weep uncontrollably. Will was taken aback that someone so young could be so sad, lonely and hurt. For the first time since the curse he felt compassion. Revenge, hatred and bitterness had been his only allies, until he met this poor little mite.

"Come along now, lad, stop all o' this hollerin'," said Will softly. "If you want to be me first mate and me friend, you're gonna have to be tough."

Johnnie lowered his hands from his face and through the sobs said, "Can I call you Captain Will?" hoping the pirate would want him as a friend.

"No, no, no, lad!" said the pirate. Johnnie's heart sank but the pirate continued, "Special people get to call me Will, so that's what you must call me, too."

"Oh, no!" Johnnie shrieked.

"What is it, boy? If you don't you want to call me Will, that's alright. Call me whatever you like!" said the pirate.

"No, no, I want to call you Will. It's just that I'm late for dinner. He'll go mad," Johnnie said, panicking, trying to think of an excuse to give Nathaniel when he got home.

"Calm down, lad. He's not going to feed you to the sharks or hang, draw and quarter you," said Will, trying to reassure Johnnie. "Just tell him you were passing the time of day with Will."

Before he could think, the words were out, "Oh yes, Will, that'll go down really well. Nathaniel will say,

'Where have you been boy?' and I'll say, 'Just passing the time of day with the local ghost'."

Will looked down at the table.

"Oh, Will. I'm so sorry; I can't believe I said that. I know you were only trying to help."

Will looked up and said softly, "That's alright, lad. I understand. Now you be off home. Go on, off you go."

"I don't want to leave you on your own, though," said Johnnie, still feeling bad about his outburst.

But Will threw his head back and laughed. "Run along, lad. I've managed on my own for nigh on two hundred years. I think I'll get through this night 'n' all. Now you get yourself off home," he said.

"Okay, but I will be here first thing in the morning," said Johnnie, smiling.

He leaped off *The Morada* and began to run as fast as his legs would carry him. It was already very dark and everything looked different now. He could hear all sorts of strange noises. He was running out of breath and could feel every beat of his heart as he sped homewards. At last he saw the lights of his house. It was time to face the music.

CHAPTER TWO
Grounded

Nathaniel met him at the front door.

"Where have you been, boy? What did I tell you? Well I hope it was worth it boy, because you're grounded for a week," roared Nathaniel, not allowing him time to answer.

Johnnie's heart sank. That meant he would not be able to see Will.

"You can't do that! No. Please, Mum, tell him he can't do that," pleaded Johnnie.

"Just go to bed, Johnnie," replied Laura, yawning.

Johnnie could feel the anger growing and taking over him. His mum never took his side.

"I hate both of you! I'm always in the way here. Neither of you can be bothered with me but I'll sort that," he screamed, and turning on his heels, he ran back into the night.

He could hear his mother shouting, "Johnnie, Johnnie, get back here!"

Nathaniel roared, "Let the brat go, he'll come whimpering back later."

Sobbing, Johnnie arrived back at *The Morada* and jumped aboard. He climbed down the stairs and sat back at the table opposite Will.

"What's the matter, lad? Come on now," Will said softly.

"My father hates me, my mother hates me and I hate Nathaniel. I don't know why Mum married him. If my father hadn't left, we'd all still be together in London and my mother would be happy."

Will looked puzzled.

"Listen, lad. Hate is a mighty strong word. No one could hate you and if they did then it'd be more fool them. Older folks make mistakes 'n' all. It just takes them a while to realise the damage they can cause. But I'll tell you something, lad. I could bet a bag of sovereigns that neither your mother nor your father hates you."

Will moved his head to the side as if he could hear something.

"Can you hear that, lad?"

"Hear what?" Johnnie asked.

"Sshh," said Will.

Johnnie listened and, realising it was his mum, scowled.

"That's my mum calling on me, Will."

Will looked at him and smiling softly said, "Sure doesn't sound like she hates you to me, lad."

"What do you mean, Will?" asked Johnnie.

"Well if I hated someone I sure wouldn't be searchin' all over Pearl Bay to make sure they were safe, now would I, lad? Now shout back to her and be sure she hears you."

Johnnie started climbing the stairs, turned and said, "I'll shout Will, but I'm not going back with her."

He could see his mother looking around the dock and calling his name.

"I'm over here," he shouted angrily. His mother turned at the sound of his voice.

"What are you playing at Johnnie? Get off that boat before you hurt yourself," she yelled, running towards the ship.

"I'm staying here, Mum," he said defiantly. "You go back to Nathaniel and live happily ever after. And it's a *ship,* not a boat."

He could tell that his mother was worried, but there was no way he was going with her. Laura moved to the side and, looking past Johnnie, she bellowed, "I don't know who you are but you better get my boy off your boat now or I'm calling the police."

Johnnie turned around and there was Will standing by the wheel. He couldn't believe it.

"Mum, you can see him! Will, she sees you!" he exclaimed, in disbelief.

Johnnie thought he was going to burst with excitement but his mother looked at him as if he were crazy.

"Have you lost your mind, Johnnie? Of course I can see him. Now get off the boat or I'm coming on," she said, moving towards the ship.

Another troubled soul, thought Will. "Go on lad, go with your mother," he said.

Johnnie couldn't believe he was taking her side.

"No way, Will, I'm not going back, ever," Johnnie replied stubbornly.

Suddenly he heard a loud thud and turned to find his mother, scrambling to her feet beside him.

"Mum, are you okay?" he asked, helping her up. Laura grabbed hold of Johnnie and held him close to her as if she would never let him go.

"I was worried sick, Johnnie. Don't ever do that to me again," she said, still clinging onto him.

Suddenly she turned on Will. "And as for you, you obviously don't have children or you would have realised the worry you have caused," she said with venom in her voice. Will turned and started to walk down the galley stairs.

"No, Will. Wait. She didn't mean it. Mum what are you doing?" said Johnnie with his hands on his head. Will disappeared into the galley.

"Come on now Johnnie, let's go. It's late and I'm tired and cold," said Laura, taking hold of Johnnie's hand.

"For the first time in your life, Mum, will you please listen to what I have to say?" he said, close to tears now.

She was startled by the pleading look in his eyes and she sat down on the side of the ship, saying simply, "Okay Johnnie I'm listening."

.He took a deep breath and told his mother everything about Will, The Devil's Son and the curse. When he had finished there was a long silence.

"Well Mum, tell me what you're thinking," asked Johnnie warily.

Laura looked at him and said, "Let me see. What do I think? I think that he's a sad man, who gets his kicks out of telling stories to children. Pretending to you he's a pirate is bad enough, but to make you feel sorry for him is sick, and I worry about what his motives are."

"I knew you wouldn't believe me, I just knew it," Johnnie said angrily, pacing up and down the deck. Then he had an idea. His eyes lit up with mischief as he said, "Okay, Mum, let's put it to the test. We'll take Will home to meet Nathaniel. If he can see him, I promise I will never go near him or the ship again."

Laura shook her head in exasperation. "Okay, Johnnie, if that is what it is going to take to convince you. But once Nathaniel sees him, I'm informing the police," she said.

"Will! Will!" yelled Johnnie.

There was no answer.

He picked his way carefully back down the rickety steps to the gloomy galley below. Will was sitting in his chair once more with his head in his hands.

"Your mother's right, lad, I was only thinking of me self. I never gave a minute's thought about her worry. Nor should I be burdening a young 'un with my woes," said Will, shaking his head.

"Will, she was angry, but we can prove it's the truth," said Johnnie hopefully.

"There's no point in it, lad. What good will it do?" he said sadly.

"That's not true, Will. You were right. My mum does love me. And if I'd never met you we wouldn't be talking or hugging again. Remember the curse, Will. You can only be seen by people as sad as you. I knew my mum was sad and really unhappy, and her seeing you proves it. Maybe we can help her if we prove your story is true. Please Will, do this for me, come back with us," pleaded Johnnie.

Will stood up slowly, "Come along then, lad, let's get this over with," he said.

"Yes! Thanks Will," said Johnnie, punching the air. Carefully, they picked their way upstairs once more.

Laura was still sitting where he had left her. "Okay Mum we're ready to go," beamed Johnnie.

Laura looked Will up and down. "Have you got everything you need Mr. Pirate? Parrot? Crutch, perhaps?"

Johnnie glared at his mum, but Will just laughed and said, "No ma'am, I'll go as I am."

They left the ship and headed for Johnnie's house. Will kept looking all around him.

"Man alive, I'd never 'ave known the island. It's all changed, lad, it's all changed," he said, shaking his head in disbelief.

"And when's the last time you walked around the island, Mr. Pirate?" asked Laura.

"His name's Will," said Johnnie, glaring at his mother again.

"That would 'ave been about two hundred years ago, ma'am," said Will, looking Laura straight in the eye.

Laura roared with laughter. "You're good. The only thing that disappoints me, though, is that you haven't said, 'Har, Har me hearties' yet. Every true pirate says that at least once in a while."

Johnnie looked at Will and said, "It's good to see her laugh again, Will."

"If you say so, lad, if you say so," replied Will, shaking his head.

Nathaniel was looking out of the window as they arrived at the house. Johnnie could feel his mouth drying up as they neared the front door. *What if mum was right and Will was lying?*

Laura opened the door and the three of them walked into the living room. Nathaniel was still fuming. "I told you to leave him out there. The little brat needs a lesson in humility. He'd have come back, grovelling. He'll have to learn that he won't get away with defiance in my home."

The colour drained from Laura's face as she looked at Will, who stood there as large as life with his arms folded across his chest, smiling and shrugging his shoulders.

"Oh my God, it's true!" she shrieked.

"Damn right it's true! And maybe next time you'll let me handle things. Could you look at me, woman, when I'm talking to you?" said Nathaniel, with his hands on his hips. Laura turned around to face him. She was still ghostly white.

"What's the matter with you, woman? You look like you've seen a ghost."

Johnnie and Will roared with laughter.

"Do you think it's funny, boy? Maybe being grounded until school starts might not be so funny. It might give you time to think about how lucky you are that I took you and your mother on," growled Nathaniel, shaking with rage.

Johnnie looked over at Will, who was shaking his head and glaring at Nathaniel.

"No!" Laura shouted.

"No? What do you mean no, woman?" Nathaniel growled.

Laura turned her back on Nathaniel and winked at Johnnie and Will. "I have an idea," she said.

"You? An idea? This I've got to hear!" sneered Nathaniel.

"You're right, Nathaniel, Johnnie does need discipline, and I think I have the answer," she said.

Johnnie couldn't believe his ears. *What on earth was she saying?*

"Give her a chance, lad," said Will calmly.

Laura continued, "There is an old ship down at the harbour. It is rotten and badly damaged. It is thought to have been a famous pirate ship years and years ago. It's called *The Morada.*"

"Hold on! Enough of the history lesson," interrupted Nathaniel, "Could we get to the point?"

Laura ignored him and went on. "If it was restored, it could be worth a lot of money to you as a pleasure ship, taking tourists on cruises around the island."

Nathaniel looked stunned. "You just might be onto something there, woman. Tourists, and kids especially, go for all that pirate legend crap. But where does the discipline for the brat come in?"

"Oh, there are lots of dirty jobs that are going to need to be done before the real restoration begins," replied Laura. "Then we'll need all hands on deck to help the restorers. Now I think that might take six weeks, at least."

"Tell him you're not working on a stinking rotten ship, lad," said Will.

What? *I can't believe he's asking me to say that.* He screwed his face up, to let Will know he didn't want to say it.

"Trust me lad. I'm a sly old fox," said Will, smiling.

Johnnie took a deep breath. "I'm not working on any stinking rotten old ship!" he said.

Nathaniel swung around. "Oh yes you will, boy! And if you don't, you'll be indoors with no television for six weeks," he growled.

Johnnie just managed to stop himself from punching the air and shouting "yes!"

"Okay, you win. I'll do it," he said meekly.

Will winked at him and rubbed his hands together.

"That's better, boy. Respect is what you're gonna learn in my house. I'm going to bed. I suggest you two do the same," sneered Nathaniel.

"We will be up in a minute. I just want to speak to Johnnie a bit more about what's expected of him," replied Laura, sternly, for Nathaniel's benefit.

As Nathaniel headed upstairs to bed, Johnnie couldn't contain himself any longer; he punched the air yelling, "Yes, yes!"

"Sshh!" Laura whispered, "You'll have Nathaniel back down. Now say goodnight to Will and go up to bed. I think you've had enough excitement for one day."

Johnnie threw his arms around his mother and said, "This is the best day ever, Mum."

Her eyes filled with tears but Johnnie knew that she was happier than she had been for a very long time.

"Hurry up and get to bed," she said, rubbing the top of his head.

"Goodnight Will, goodnight Mum. See you in the morning," whispered Johnnie. Then, bounding out of the room he took the stairs two at a time.

Will and Laura went outside and stood on the path.

"I really don't know where to begin, Will. I am so sorry I mocked you. I must have sounded so cruel. It has all been just too much to take in. I am so, so confused," said Laura.

"It's alright ma'am. Nothin' to fret over," interrupted Will. "Not every day you meet a real live ghost pirate, so to speak. That's a mighty fine lad you have there, you know," he went on.

Laura lowered her head and sighed, "I know, and I have let him down so badly. I was so wrapped up in self-pity that I forgot he had lost his father and needed me more than ever," she said, looking up into the sky.

"Johnnie's father and I divorced a few years ago," she said.

"He must have been a few tot's o' rum short o' a bottle to let someone as pretty as you go, ma'am," replied Will, chortling.

Suddenly the bedroom window flew open and Nathaniel's head appeared. "What on earth is going on out there, woman? Have you lost your mind? Standing alone talking to yourself?"

"Sorry I disturbed you, Nathaniel. I'm just coming in," she said.

"So you should be. It seems like you and your boy have both lost your minds at the same time," he said as he slammed the window shut and drew the curtains again.

"I'd better go in now. Thanks, Will," whispered Laura.

"Thanks for what, ma'am?" asked Will.

"For helping me to realise just how much I love my son. See you tomorrow. Oh, and one other thing, I'm not the Queen of England, so you can call me Laura," she said smiling.

As she walked into the house and closed the door quietly behind her, Will turned and headed back down the path. Suddenly he jumped into the air and clicked his heels. For the first time since the curse, he was looking forward to the dawning of a new day.

CHAPTER THREE
Money Matters

Johnnie was up bright and early the next day as he couldn't wait to see Will. He washed and changed quickly and was about to go down to breakfast when he stopped in his tracks. *What am I doing? If Nathaniel thinks I'm enjoying the thought of going to work on an old boat, he won't see it as a punishment and will keep me indoors.* He undressed and jumped back into bed. Before long Nathaniel came barging into his room.

"Up you get, boy. You've work to do. No time for lazing around!"

Johnnie pulled the covers down from his face and whining, replied, "Oh no! Do I have to?"

Nathaniel glared at him and said angrily,

"Yes, you damn well do. Didn't you listen to a damn word I said yesterday, boy?"

Slowly, Johnnie got out of bed and, slouching, walked at a snail's pace towards the bathroom.

"Move, boy. Your mother hasn't got all day to wait on you," growled Nathaniel.

Johnnie locked the bathroom door and chuckled to himself in front of the mirror.

"One nil to me," he whispered at his reflection.

He quickly got washed and dressed, then headed down to breakfast.

"You're late Johnnie," said Laura, winking.

He finished his breakfast, washed his dishes and was soon ready to go.

"Are you ready to go, Nathaniel?" asked Laura. He looked up from his paper.

"Go where, woman?" he asked, his face twisting with annoyance.

"To start cleaning the ship and maybe to talk to some restorers on the island about prices for materials," she replied.

Nathaniel looked at her blankly. "Have you gone completely mad, woman? I can't go on no rotten old ship with my bronchitis the way it is. Anyhow it's me that's paying for it all. The organ grinder don't do menial," laughed Nathaniel as he buried his face in the paper again.

"Come on Johnnie, let's get going," said Laura, shaking her head. *What goes around comes around.*

"It's okay, Mum, we don't need him anyway. We'll have better fun without him," said Johnnie, as they set off.

"That's enough Johnnie. Don't let me hear you talking about Nathaniel like that," Laura replied sternly. "I was only trying to—"

"Look, Johnnie, just forget about it."

They walked the remainder of the journey in silence. Johnnie was confused. *Why is she defending him when he's been so nasty to her?* As they neared *The Morada* Laura was the first to break the silence.

"Oh my God," said Laura, with a stunned look on her face.

"What is it Mum? Are you okay?" said Johnnie, thinking he had upset her.

Laura stared at the ship in disbelief. "I hadn't realised what a state it was in. No wonder no one else on the island has tried to restore it. It will cost a fortune to repair all that damage."

"But Mum, you saw it last night and it was your idea to fix it up," he said, anxious now that she might change her mind.

Laura stared at the ship and shook her head, "Yes, Johnnie, I saw it last night but it was pitch dark. I couldn't see half of the damage."

Johnnie lowered his head.

"So we won't be able to fix it up, then?" he said softly.

He looked so forlorn.

"Don't give up just yet," she said. "We'll speak to the local contractors and get quotes. The difficult bit may be convincing Nathaniel that it would be worth his while to restore it as a pleasure ship." *I have to try; this means so much to him.*

"Morning, folks," boomed a voice that Johnnie had been longing to hear since he woke up. He turned around and there was Will standing on the deck.

"Good morning," they replied in unison, grinning from ear to ear.

"And a mighty fine morning it is, too," said Will, with a glint in his eye.

"There's a lot more damage than I first thought, Will," said Laura quietly.

"Well she's an old girl now, ma'am. How do you think you'll look if you ever reach the ripe old age of two hundred years?" laughed Will.

"True," chuckled Laura.

"Anyway we have to have an idea as to what she looked like in her former glory, so we can get a price for restoration," said Laura, scratching her head.

"If I tells you what she looked like, then one of you could draw her," replied Will.

"Johnnie, you're good at drawing, do you think you could do that?" asked Laura.

"I could try, Mum, but I don't have any paper or pencils," said Johnnie.

Laura took twenty dollars from her jeans pocket. "You'd better go and get what you need then," she said. "I'm coming aboard, Will."

She took a long run and launched herself onto the ship. Smiling at Will, she picked herself up and said,

"I'm getting quite good at this."

Will looked at her in disbelief, "Aye, Laura you're a tough 'un. I wouldn't be fancying coming home a sovereign short to you," he said.

"I wish I was tough, but I'm not. If I was, this is the last place I'd be," she said.

"If me manners are letting me down, just tell me Laura, but why Nathaniel? He treats you and the lad no better than dogs."

Laura's eyes filled with tears as she began, "It all started to go downhill for us when Johnnie's father disappeared. Joe was always the life and soul of the party, he brightened up the room just by being there. People loved him, but not half as much as I did. When things were going wrong he always knew how to cheer me up. I found it impossible to be angry with him. But he was a dreamer; he always promised me he would build me a mansion and smother me with diamonds. Neither of those things were important to me; I was happy with the way life was. We were comfortable and had money in the bank. I didn't need to work and could stay at home with Johnnie. Everything was fine; at least I thought so. Joe liked to put a wager on the horses, but it never bothered me because he told me it was only a couple of pounds. He worked hard, so I didn't mind. One night he never came home. I was panic-stricken. I phoned his friends but no one had seen him. I contacted the hospitals but he hadn't been admitted. The police couldn't do anything and told me he'd probably turn up soon, wondering what all the fuss was about. I contacted Joe's employers first thing in the morning to see if they knew anything."

Laura paused momentarily then continued, "They informed me that he had called the day before to say he was ill and wouldn't be in for the rest of the week. I couldn't take in what was being said. I told them that they must have made a mistake, but they assured me they hadn't. I dropped Johnnie off at a neighbour's and spent hours searching all the places in town I thought he could be. No one had seen or heard from him. When I returned home there was a moving van sitting outside the house. I opened the front door but when I went to close it behind me it wouldn't shut. I turned around to find two burly men standing on the doorstep. One of them had put his foot in the doorway to stop me from closing the door. The pair of them barged past me and were soon joined by a third seedy little character. The first two started taking the furniture out of the house. I couldn't believe what was happening. I tried to stop them, but the third man pushed me out of the way. I told them to leave my house immediately or I would telephone the police. The little man took a piece of paper out of his pocket and grinning, gave it to me. At last - an explanation. I was convinced that they had made some sort of mistake. They must be at the wrong house. I unfolded the paper quickly, my heart pounding, and began to read.

"The paper turned out to be an IOU and it was signed by Joe. He had signed away the contents of our home to pay off a gambling debt, which he owed to Sammy McIntosh, a bookmaker with a bad reputation for violence. There was no mistake. All I could do was stand by and watch as they emptied our beautiful home of the furniture I had so lovingly collected and cared for over the years. Sofas, tables, chairs, rugs, pictures, clocks – all were unceremoniously bundled into the back of the van. One of the men must have had a pang of conscience. 'Look,' he said, 'we've left you and the boy your beds. Don't make a big deal about this. Sammy can be a very nasty piece of work.' I had heard of Sammy's reputation for being vicious and nasty. I was distraught. I stood for a while looking at the empty living room. By the time I reached the bank, I suppose I was already beginning to realise that there would be no money in the account. Sure enough, Joe had withdrawn every penny the previous day.

"I've wracked my brains ever since about why I didn't see it coming, but I never suspected for one moment that he was in that kind of trouble. He never gave me any indication that he was in trouble. To top it all, he hadn't paid any of the bills for months. Final demands for payment had been sent out but he never told me. He dealt with the money and the bills, so I was oblivious to what was going on. Eventually I got a job but I still couldn't make ends meet. We were about to lose the house and…"

"That's why you married Nathaniel," said Will, interrupting.

Laura continued. "Nathaniel used to come into the café where I worked and have lunch. One day I broke down in the café and poured my heart out to a colleague about my predicament. Nathaniel had been in the café and overheard the conversation. He approached me the next day with a proposition. Nathaniel explained that he had been left a vast sum of money by a rich aunt but had to be married in order to claim his inheritance. He stated that if I married him he would clear my debts and buy a home for us in America. I was to sign an agreement stating that if I ever left him I would walk away with nothing. He made it clear that if I contested the document after we were married, he would disappear, leaving Johnnie and myself to fend for ourselves in a new country. I had no relatives or friends that I could turn to, so after weeks of soul searching and more demands from creditors, I decided to marry him. I signed his agreement and we were married quietly in a local registry office. Johnnie sat scowling through the whole façade, bewildered as to why I would marry this man. And the rest as they say, is history."

"There you see now; I was right, Laura," said Will, "You're one gutsy lady. To go through what you've been through for the sake of the lad takes a lot a guts. I know how it feels to live without love and I know what I'd rather have. But one day, Laura, for every time you've been wronged, you'll receive a blessing, and by God, our maker will be busy that day."

"Your family must have really loved you," she said.

"You can but hope, ma'am, you can but hope," replied Will.

Suddenly there was a loud thud. They turned around to find Johnnie scrambling to his feet, armed with a large pad of paper and a handful of coloured pencils.

"Are you goin' to be drawin' a fleet of ships lad?" laughed Will.

"Yes, are you sure you have enough there?" asked Laura.

"I wanted to make sure I had enough so I didn't have to go all the way back," laughed Johnnie.

He sat down on the deck with his paper and pencils and began to draw as Will explained in detail how the ship had been in her heyday. Laura watched them laugh and argue as a picture of *The Morada* gradually took shape.

When the drawing was finally finished, Will's eyes welled with tears as he looked at it.

"A more beautiful sight I've never seen, lad. Present company excepted of course, ma'am," said Will.

"Johnnie, it's so long since I've seen you draw, that I'd forgotten just how good you are," said Laura, beaming with pride. "This is just absolutely wonderful." She hugged Johnnie and kissed the top of his head.

"I'd do the same lad, if I could. You've made an old pirate very happy," said Will, purring with contentment.

The next three hours were spent going around the island talking to boat builders about restoring *The Morada*. None of them was interested in the work. They wouldn't even go down to the ship to give an estimate of the cost of repairing it. They just said they couldn't take it on, but no reason was given. With one last boat-builder to try, Laura and Johnnie were beginning to lose hope. *Why does no one want to take it on? Surely someone needs the work?*

They were very quiet as Laura knocked on the door of the last workshop. The man who answered was tall with tousled fair hair, which didn't look as if it had seen a comb that day. He had a friendly weather-beaten face and the kind of blue eyes which always looked as though they were laughing.

"What can I do you for?" he asked.

"You are our last hope," said Laura. "I'm looking for a builder to restore the old ship in the harbour, but so far I haven't even been able to get anyone to go near it, never mind give me a quote for repairs."

"Now would that be *The Morada* you're talking about?" the man asked.

"Yes, that's the one," said Laura anxiously.

He stepped out into the sunshine shaking his head.

"You won't get anybody from around here to go near her," he laughed. "Legend has it that she's cursed, and that all her crew were killed at sea by The Devil's Son."

"So I take it that you won't consider the job either, then?" she said sharply.

"Oh, I've never been one to turn down work," he said, wiping his hands with a rag, "but there's a lot of work involved in that old lady."

Laura's heart skipped a beat. "But why would *you* do it?" she asked, trying not to frighten him off.

The man laughed, "Oh, I'm not from around these parts. I've only just moved here with my new wife. I also have an ex-wife and two kids to support."

Laura and Johnnie grabbed each other and started jumping for joy around the yard.

"Hold on! You haven't seen my price yet," chuckled the man.

"Would you come down to the harbour and give me an estimate today?" pleaded Laura.

"You don't ask for much, do you?" said the man, shaking his head.

"Please," replied Laura, "we'd like to get things moving as quickly as possible."

"Oh, I suppose so. Just give me two minutes to get myself organised," he replied, heading back into his workshop.

Back on board *The Morada,* Johnnie showed the man his drawing and explained what they were hoping for. The man had a good look around, measuring and prodding this and that and scribbling notes as he went along. After a while he sat down on the side of the ship to do a few calculations. Laura couldn't contain herself any longer.

"What do you think?" she asked. "Remember Johnnie and I will be here every day helping as well." She hoped it would make a difference to the price. There was a long silence. He didn't appear to be listening.

"What I can't understand," he said, scratching his head in disbelief, "is that considering her age, she's not as bad as she looks. The hull is fine and the damage is mostly superficial, from a builder's perspective, that is. I just can't understand the condition she's in considering the length of time she's been in the water with no maintenance of any kind. However, materials are still expensive. I would say with the wood, sails, treatments, masts, labour and the like, you'd be looking at fifty thousand, minimum."

Laura slumped onto the side of the ship. "Nathaniel will never go for that," she said.

"I'm sorry, but I can't cut corners on a thing like this. She has to be seaworthy. But I promise you one thing… For that price she will look as good as she did on the day she made her maiden voyage and she will have the advantage of being motorised, so she won't be as dependent on the weather as she was in those days. She will be much easier to sail. And don't forget, this will be an investment. People will be queuing to the end of the harbour to sail on her. The legend will be all the publicity you need to attract the tourists. Companies will pay top dollar to hire pleasure boats for corporate hospitality."

Laura had listened intently and was beginning to feel much better about the prospect of Nathaniel giving the go-ahead for the project.

"I think you just might be right. It all depends on how well we sell this to Nathaniel, and I think I may just have an idea about that," she said with a devilish glint in her eye.

"Listen, my name's Gerry. If you have any questions or you want to go ahead, here's my card. But I will need to know quickly so I can organise my work crew. I'm gonna need the best men for this job."

He shook hands with Laura. "I'm sorry, I must get back. I've a job on at the moment and it has to be finished tonight," he said before heading back.

Johnnie and Will sat with their heads in their hands.

"There's no way Nathaniel will pay fifty thousand dollars, Mum. You know what he's like with money," moaned Johnnie.

"He will if he thinks he is going to outdo someone and make a handsome profit along the way. Just you leave it to me," said Laura, looking extremely pleased with herself.

"I do believe your mother has a plan, lad," Will chortled.

"We'd better be getting off home, Johnnie," said Laura. "Rub your hands along the side of the ship and wipe them on your face. We've got to make Nathaniel think you've been working."

"Slyer than an old fox you are. I wouldn't 'ave liked to pit my wits against you," said Will, laughing.

They headed off, shouting their goodbyes to Will, but had only got a few hundred yards down the road when Will appeared beside them.

"Sorry folks but I just couldn't contain meself. I just have to witness old Nathaniel being out-foxed. Do you mind?"

Johnnie and Laura just laughed and they all continued on their way.

. They got home to find Nathaniel, mouth open, snoring on the settee. He woke up with a start. "God damn it. What are you pair sneaking around at? Is dinner ready yet, woman?"

Will shook his head and Laura took a deep breath.

"We've just arrived from the boat yard this minute," said Laura, trying to contain her annoyance.

"So, how did you get on, woman?" said Nathaniel, placing his hands on his hips.

"I checked around all the boatyards, but somebody has already approached them and is prepared to pay forty-five thousand dollars to turn it into a pleasure ship for corporate hires. Seemingly, they'll pay top dollar, especially with its legend status on the island. I told them to forget it - forty-five thousand dollars, indeed. Who has that kind of money?"

"Have you lost your mind? Do you know how much a ship like that could make me? Since when do you make my decisions, woman?"

"Well I just thought it was a lot of money, Nathaniel, but they did say that if they were offered fifty thousand they could start work right away."

"We'll be down there first thing tomorrow morning and steal a march on the opposition. The early bird catches the worm. I should have stuck to my rule. Never send a woman to do a man's work."

Laura winked at Johnnie and Will as she headed into the kitchen to prepare dinner.

"Your mother's a mighty smart woman, lad. Fit for any man," said Will, staring into the kitchen with an air of melancholy about him. "Anyways, I'd better be off and leave you in peace," he said, looking decidedly confused, "I'll see you tomorrow, lad."

It had been a long time since Johnnie had felt this happy, yet as Will left he couldn't help noticing that he was much quieter than usual. He wondered if ghosts get tired.

Nathaniel woke Laura and Johnnie very early the next day.

"Come on, you two, no time for lazing around. I've a deal to close."

In no time at all they were all heading for the boat yard.

"Listen up, woman, I don't want you screwing this up, so let me do the talking," he said. Laura nodded.

When they arrived at Gerry's workshop the sign over the intercom said, "Please ring and wait." Nathaniel held his finger on the bell for some time. There was a crackling sound as the intercom came to life.

"Just a moment! I'll be right with you," said a voice from within.

Impatient, Nathaniel banged on the door. It swung open and Gerry appeared.

"Jesus, is there a fire?" he said, glaring at Nathaniel. Then, noticing Laura and Johnnie standing behind this rude man, his face broke into a smile.

"Hey, how are you folks doin'?" he beamed, stepping out of the workshop into the sunlight.

"I'm Nathaniel Banks. My wife here tells me you've been offered forty-five thousand dollars to restore *The Morada* and kit her out as a pleasure cruiser. I'm here to offer you fifty thousand to do the work for *me*," said Nathaniel. "What do you say? Do we have a deal?"

Gerry sneaked a look at Laura and saw her give him a wink behind Nathaniel's back.

"Sure," said Gerry, holding out his hand to seal the deal. Nathaniel ignored the proffered hand and went on.

"I'll be funding this restoration personally, so all decisions will be made by me and me alone. Understood?"

Gerry looked at Laura. "Understood," he said, eyeing Nathaniel with contempt.

"Right!" nodded Nathaniel, "Now let's see what I'm restoring."

"You haven't seen it yet?" Gerry looked amused. *This should be good.*

As they neared *The Morada*, Johnnie and Laura could see Will standing

36

on the deck, looking out at the ocean. Nathaniel gazed open-mouthed at *The Morada*.

"I have never in my life seen anything so ugly," he said.

"You'll have to buy your man a looking glass, Laura," shouted Will from the deck.

"You reckon I can make some money from this floating garbage?" said Nathaniel, glowering at Gerry.

"Pots of it," replied Gerry.

Nathaniel stood without saying a word for what seemed like an eternity.

"I'll give you forty thousand up front and ten thousand on completion," he said eventually.

Gerry held out a rough brown hand, "You might just have a deal," he said.

"On one condition," said Nathaniel. "The work has to be completed in six weeks. I'm looking for a quick return on my investment. If you finish the job on time you get the ten thousand, and I'll employ any of your crew in need of work as deck hands. If you don't finish on time, I keep the money and the offer of employment is null and void. Now, you either want the job or you don't."

"Six weeks?" said Gerry, scratching his head. His financial situation wasn't looking too great at the moment and he felt responsible for his crew. They relied on him. He sighed, "Alright, it's a done deal. I'll need you to fill out some forms, later. The ship has to be registered. It's only three hundred dollars, but it keeps everything legal. I'll organise my crew and we'll start tomorrow." The two men shook hands.

"Right, there's work to be done," said Nathaniel, rubbing his hands together and looking at Johnnie and Laura, "Don't just stand there. My man here will tell you what you need to do," he said. As he turned on his heels and headed homewards whistling happily to himself, they all stared after him in total disbelief. It was Gerry who broke the uncomfortable silence.

"I'm sorry, I know he's your husband an' all but he's the most unlikeable person I've ever encountered."

Laura shrugged her shoulders.

"Well, Johnnie, let's get on board and see what we can do to get started," she said, changing the subject.

"I'm gonna get going," shouted Gerry. "I've got a lot of organising to do. The first thing to be done tomorrow is to get a gangplank erected so that you two can walk aboard. I don't want two of my best crew missing work with broken legs," he said, laughing.

Laura and Johnnie joined Will, who had been standing watching everything that had been going on with great interest.

"It's happening, Will. It's really going to happen. *The Morada* will be the best ship on the sea again," said Johnnie, grinning.

"Aye, we'll see lad, we'll see," replied Will.

Laura asked Johnnie to start by gathering up all the old pieces of wood that were lying around. She and Will watched together as he darted to and fro around the deck. Will seemed a little subdued, but when she asked him if he was alright, he replied simply, "Just dandy, ma'am, just dandy."

"Will, I'm so sorry about all the horrible things that have happened to you. I know that it may not be much comfort, but if it weren't for you, Johnnie and I would have drifted further and further apart. I've haven't seen him this happy in a long time, and I wouldn't want anything to spoil that."

Will nodded in understanding.

"Johnnie, you haven't put a flag on her," shouted Will, laughing.

"A flag, Will? What do you mean?"

"She was a pirate ship lad, she has to have a pirate flag," said Will, pointing to Johnnie's drawing of *The Morada*. Johnnie immediately stopped what he had been doing.

"You're right, Will, but I'll sort that right now," he said, and proceeded to draw in the missing flag.

"What do you think, Will?" he asked, holding up the drawing.

"Now that really is *The Morada*, lad," he said, smiling at Johnnie.

Laura looked over to Will, clasped her hands around her mouth and mouthed the words, "Thank you."

They spent the rest of the day in high spirits, laughing and listening to Will as he recounted tales of his adventures on the high seas, until it was time to head home for dinner.

"Do you mind if an old pirate accompanies you, ma'am?" asked Will, smiling.

"That would be an honour, kind sir," replied Laura, giggling.

They were still laughing when they arrived at the gate of the house. Nathaniel was there to meet them. "Don't look like you two have done much in the way of work. There's not a lick of dirt on either of you," he said sneering.

"We lifted all the old wood and stacked it up," replied Johnnie.

"I ain't talking to you, boy. When are you gonna learn to speak only when you're spoken to?" snapped Nathaniel.

"Lay off the lad and match yerself with me," said Will angrily, but Nathaniel, oblivious to his presence, continued his speech.

"I've paid the first sum of money to that Gerry character and organised an eight a.m. start for you two tomorrow. I've also signed about a million papers so the ship could be registered. I've never seen so much paperwork. Anyway it's done now except for one thing. I don't know why, but it seems that because you're my spouse, you have to witness my signature on the forms and sign them, too. I think you could just about manage that, so Gerry will bring the forms with him to the ship tomorrow."

Will was seething with rage at the way Nathaniel had spoken to Laura and Johnnie. *One day! One day!* he thought, glaring at Nathaniel's retreating back.

"I'd better be off then folks. Now be sure and get a good night's sleep. We've lots to do in the morning," he said as he headed back to *The Morada*.

Laura and Johnnie were up and out of the house the next morning before Nathaniel awoke. They arrived at *The Morada* to find trucks, hoists and workers everywhere.

A smiling Gerry greeted them. "Morning, folks. Fit and ready to start?" he asked, directing his crew to their designated areas.

"I've never seen so many machines," said Laura in disbelief.

"It's a big job," replied Gerry. "We were lucky, though. There's not much work around at the minute, so we got the plant cheap."

Johnnie could see Will scratching his head, and looking in wonder at all the activity and strange machinery that was around him.

"Oh, and before I forget, Laura could you sign these two forms?" said Gerry. "And could you also print your name and address at the top there?"

"Is that all you need?" she replied, obviously more interested in all that was going on around her.

"That'll do nicely," he answered.

As promised, the new gangplank was now in place and Gerry set Johnnie and Laura a few tasks for the day before heading off to supervise his crew.

Will kept a careful eye on proceedings as Johnnie and Laura set about the tasks that Gerry had given them. They became so engrossed in the work that it was beginning to get dark before they knew it.

Suddenly Nathaniel appeared.

"Any slower, boy, and you'll have stopped," he bellowed at one of Gerry's crew. With a steely glare the man stood up and walked towards Nathaniel.

Gerry jumped in between the pair and gesturing to the man said. "Right, Chuck, take five!"

He pulled Nathaniel to one side and spoke to him quietly through gritted teeth. "Next time you interfere with my crew like that I won't save your miserable skin. I'll take my crew off site and you can find someone else to do your lousy job," he said fuming.

"Hold on now, Gerry! Don't take things so seriously," Nathaniel blustered.

"You've already laid down your stipulations," said Gerry in a calm and measured tone, "now you listen to mine. One, you don't talk to my crew. Two, you only come near the ship at the end of the day and three, I'm in charge, so any information you want, you get directly from me. Take it or leave it!"

Nathaniel looked ready to explode.

"Hey, if that's the way you want it, no problem. But it had better be finished in time or you'll find yourself out of pocket," he replied, sneering.

With a satisfied smile, Will had watched the proceedings. *Nathaniel needs a good thrashing. I only wish I could do it meself, but Gerry won't take any nonsense from him.*

"Right, men. You've done a good job. That'll do us for today," said Gerry.

✳ ✳ ✳ ✳ ✳

Five weeks of furious activity had gone by. Nathaniel had stuck to the rules, but had made a point of complaining to Gerry every day about one thing or another. Laura and Johnnie had worked their fingers to the bone and Gerry's men had done a magnificent job of restoring *The Morada* to her former glory.

One day, after the crew had gone home, Johnnie, Will and Laura stood looking around them at what had been achieved. "This is a sight I never could 'ave imagined," said Will, his eyes filling with tears.

"I'm just an old fool," he said, "enough of this now. It's a joyous time and at joyous times we sing and we dance." He began jigging, and singing, hands on hips, around the ship.

Laura and Johnnie joined in until suddenly Laura shrieked, "Oh no, look at the time, Johnnie! Nathaniel will be expecting his dinner. Let's get going. We've had a great day, Will. We'll see you tomorrow."

They ran down the gangplank together but suddenly Johnnie stopped and went back.

"See you tomorrow, Will. I love you," he said, before turning on his heels to catch up with Laura again. Will was speechless. He had never expected to hear those words again. Delighted, he continued to sing and jig around the ship. *Aye this has been a great day.*

CHAPTER FOUR
The Servants

When Laura and Johnnie arrived home, they found Nathaniel dressed in a blue blazer with gold buttons, a white shirt, a cravat, white trousers and a captain's hat. He was walking around puffing a cigar.

"Captain Nathaniel Banks. It has a certain ring to it, woman, don't you think?" he said.

Laura looked at him blankly.

"Don't worry, woman, I have outfits for you and the boy," said Nathaniel, reaching into a big plastic bag. He pulled out a white shirt, black knickerbockers and black shoes, and threw them to Johnnie. Next he pulled out a long dress with puffy sleeves and an apron and threw them to Laura. They stared at the outfits in disbelief.

"And what exactly are we supposed to do with these?" asked Laura.

"When I'm taking guests out on *The Morada*, you and the boy will wear these to serve the food and drinks. You've got to capture the atmosphere, woman! These outfits are authentic," said Nathaniel, puffing on his cigar.

"No way!" they chimed in unison, looking at each other in horror.

"I saved you and your boy from the gutter," roared Nathaniel through gritted teeth, "If it weren't for me you would be out on the street. Now I don't know what's gotten into you lately, woman, but you're beginning to get ideas above your station. So unless you and your boy want to head straight back to the gutter, you'd better try these outfits on."

Laura would have loved to tell Nathaniel what to do with his stupid outfits. How she wished she could have taken Johnnie away, but where could she go with no money and no place to stay? She gathered the clothes in her arms.

"Come on, Johnnie," she said quietly, and headed upstairs to get changed.

Johnnie looked at his mother in disbelief. *I can't believe she's going to let Nathaniel get away with this.*

The outfits were not a good fit on either of them. Johnnie's was too small and he could barely do the buttons up. Laura's dress was too big and they both felt utterly ridiculous. They complained bitterly to Nathaniel when they eventually ventured back downstairs.

"Nonsense," he said, "they're fine. And who do you think is going to be looking that closely at you pair, anyway? I think I'm onto a winner here. One week to go until the first cruise, and from then on, I'll be swimming in greenbacks." He rubbed his hands in glee.

Johnnie ran upstairs to his room, where he remained for the rest of the evening. Laura went in to speak to him, but he was sullen and withdrawn. Eventually she turned out his light, leaned over him, and whispered, "I know you don't understand right now, but one day you will. The most important thing you need to know is that I love you, more than anything in this world."

"I know, and I love you too, Mum, but why do we have to wear those stupid outfits?"

The next morning when they came down for breakfast, Nathaniel was already up and on the phone.

"Hey, that's great," he was saying, "nothing like a bit of publicity. I'll see you there at eleven a.m. Goodbye."

"Get into those outfits; we have a publicity shoot in an hour," he said, excitedly puffing on his fat cigar.

"Publicity shoot?" said Laura. "But *The Morada's* not finished yet. We'll just get in the way."

"Let me worry about Gerry and his crew. Just go and get into those outfits as fast as you can," he barked.

Nathaniel was wearing the captain's uniform when they came back downstairs. Laura and Johnnie walked two paces behind him as he rushed to the harbour. Will, Gerry and the crew looked on open-mouthed as the three of them arrived at *The Morada* and walked up the gangplank.

"Morning, Gerry, morning men," said Nathaniel, looking enormously pleased with himself. Laura and Johnnie looked decidedly uncomfortable, as they stood beside him in their ill-fitting outfits.

"I need a small favour, Gerry," said Nathaniel. "I have some people arriving shortly to do some publicity shots for the local papers. Would you mind if they came aboard?"

Gerry looked at Laura and Johnnie and glared at Nathaniel, barely able to hide his contempt.

"If you want to play captain, go right ahead. But just remember I have a schedule to keep to. I don't want you or your publicity people getting in the way. They can take the shots from the shore." Gerry patted Johnnie on the head and smiled at Laura. "We have a ship to finish," he said as he headed off, yelling orders to this one and that.

Nathaniel was seething but he knew that he already had reservations for cruises on *The Morada* and didn't want to run the risk of Gerry and his crew downing tools, so he yelled to Gerry's retreating back, "No problem, Gerry, we can take the pictures on the quayside with the ship in the background."

A car pulled up alongside *The Morada* just as they came down the gangplank, and two young blonde-haired girls in skimpy swimsuits jumped out. A large man carrying a camera followed them.

"Welcome to *The Morada,* a floating museum, where passengers will be able to re-capture the mystery and atmosphere of a genuine pirate ship," said Nathaniel, smiling and puffing on his cigar.

As if scripted, the girls placed themselves on either side of Nathaniel, tilted their heads onto his shoulders and gazed into his eyes. Nathaniel put his arms around their waists.

"Lovely, that's it. Hold it there. That's great. Just one more," said the photographer, snapping away with his camera. "Can we have you two in the next shot?" he asked, motioning Johnnie and Laura to join Nathaniel and the girls.

"Ah, my galley staff, of course," said Nathaniel, waving Johnnie and Laura over.

Will was angry. "Why you unworthy dog," he roared in Nathaniel's face, "if I wasn't cursed, I'd 'ave your hide."

"Alright, big smiles, big smiles," said the photographer. "The photographs will be in all the local papers next week, along with prices and the other information you gave me about the cruises, Captain."

Nathaniel looked decidedly pleased with himself as he walked the photographer and the models back to their car. He waved them off and headed homewards, puffing on his cigar without a word to anyone.

When he had left, Johnnie and Laura joined Gerry on board *The Morada.*

"Well, what do you think, Laura? She's dammed near finished. Look at her, we've brought alive a piece of history," said Gerry, cheerfully.

"She's looking just as good as you said she would, Gerry."

"She certainly is," said Will sadl., "She's looking as good as the first day I sailed in her."

"What plans have you got for tomorrow, folks?" asked Gerry.

"None really," replied Laura.

"Well in that case, would you care to cruise the island aboard *The Morada*?" said Gerry smiling.

"Is she ready?" exclaimed Johnnie.

"I sure hope so. Drowning ain't on my agenda," laughed Gerry.

Will did one of his little jigs. He knew he wasn't the best dancer in the world but it made Laura laugh and he would have done anything just to hear the sound of her laughter.

Early the next morning, Laura and Johnnie left the house without waking Nathaniel. They shut the gate quietly behind them, and ran towards the harbour. When they arrived at *The Morada* they found Will looking on in admiration as Gerry and his crew were hoisting the sails.

"Are we all ready, folks? Then let me show you this lady in action," shouted Gerry.

There was a flurry of activity and before Johnnie and Laura knew what was happening they had set sail. Will smiled with the contentment of a man who knew he was finally back where he belonged. Gerry explained to Laura that as well as having sails, *The Morada* was now motorised and therefore didn't depend on the whims of the winds, as she would have when she was first built. He showed her how to operate the engine and how to steer her. Laura couldn't believe that she was actually sailing her so easily. Will was amazed at the new *Morada*. She was even faster than before. He looked on with approval as Gerry encouraged Johnnie to take his turn at the wheel.

"You'd better enjoy this while you can, Johnnie. I can't see Nathaniel letting us sail her," said Laura.

"Oh, I don't know, sometimes life has a strange way of working things out," said Gerry, smiling.

"What do you mean?" Laura asked.

"Time will tell, Laura, time will tell," he said.

He turned the boat around and headed back to shore. Laura was still mulling over his words when she noticed Nathaniel pacing up and down on the quayside. They dropped anchor and went ashore.

"What the hell do you think you're doing?" Nathaniel roared as they dropped anchor.

"Oh just checking that she's seaworthy," said Gerry. "What did you think I was doing?"

"You took the ship out on her first voyage without, *me*, the *owner*!" Nathaniel raged.

"Hey when I'm in charge of a job, I make the decisions and I decided it would be better to test her today, than wait to see if she sunk next week, with a whole lot of tourists on her," Gerry replied.

Nathaniel reached into his pocket and handed Gerry a cheque.

"You and your crew are no longer required. It's my ship, so I make all the decisions," he said.

"And what about the launch next week? Who's going to sail her for you? And what about the crew? You promised you would keep them on when the work was finished."

"The launch has all been arranged. I won't be needing you or your men, I'm afraid," said Nathaniel, gloating.

Gerry was spitting with rage. "You told me there'd be jobs for my crew," he said, grabbing Nathaniel by the lapels.

"I had a change of heart," sneered Nathaniel, "Now get your hands off me, or I'll report you to the police for assault. Just imagine what effect that would have on your nautical licence."

Gerry let him go and walked away laughing. "Let's go lads. He's not worth the trouble. You'll get work. You can't keep good men down."

He's taking all of this rather well, thought Laura, as Gerry smiled and winked at her and Johnnie. *What can he be up to?*

"Nathaniel, that's not fair. You promised those men jobs. You can't just change your mind to get back at Gerry," she said, with concern in her voice.

"My business affairs are none of your damned concern, woman. Now just you remember your place and you'll get along fine," said Nathaniel through gritted teeth.

"He's lower than a snake's belly, Laura. You and the lad would be better off without him. Why don't you leave him and take the lad with you?" pleaded Will. "I'll look out for you."

There were tears in Laura's eyes as she smiled at Will but she took Johnnie's hand and they walked home behind Nathaniel. Johnnie looked back as they left and the tears that Will saw in his eyes made him feel distraught and totally helpless. He understood why Laura followed Nathaniel but the look in Johnnie's eyes was unbearable. *What good would I be to them, anyway?*

On the day of the launch Nathaniel was already up practising his speech when Laura and Johnnie came downstairs. It should have been a day to rejoice but they sat with their outfits on, praying for it to be over.

"You two needn't think you're going to spoil this day for me. I have a ship full of paying customers to entertain and you'd better have smiles on your sorry faces by the time we reach *The Morada*," warned Nathaniel, his voice full of malice.

As they approached the harbour, they could see that it was full of people taking photographs.

"Heed my warning!" he said through gritted teeth, before walking off to mingle with the crowd gathered on the quayside.

He's quite the entrepreneur, Laura was thinking, when suddenly she felt a hand on her shoulder.

"Good morning and happy birthday," said a familiar voice.

She turned around to find Gerry holding out a brown envelope.

"Gerry, it's good to see you, but it's not my birthday," she replied.

"Well if it ain't your birthday and it's not Christmas, it may just be a day for celebration anyway. Here, open the envelope," he said, smiling.

Laura opened the envelope. Inside were two official-looking documents.

"It's the registration forms for *The Morada*," she said. "You'd better give these to Nathaniel, Gerry."

"Look at the signatures, Laura," he said.

"Yes, they are ours," she replied, totally bemused.

"What does it say next to the signatures?" Gerry said, laughing.

"Registered owner, Laura Banks, and witness…" Puzzled, Laura stopped and went over the forms again.

"There must have been some kind of mix-up when *The Morada* was registered," she said. "This is obviously a mistake."

Gerry smiled and shook his head. "I knew as soon as I laid eyes on him that Nathaniel was a man who would go back on his word. I've watched the way he's treated you and the boy and how hard you've both worked, while he played captain. The way he's let my men down is disgraceful, but it comes as no great shock to me. On the day I registered *The Morada*, I made a pile of forms up on the computer, printed them off and put the real registration forms at the bottom. By the time he reached the real documents, Nathaniel had lost interest and just wanted the whole thing over and done with. He didn't have a clue he'd signed as a witness to *your* signature. So legally, the ship's yours, Laura. Just look at it as a wedding present from Nathaniel. I don't suppose he bothered to give you one at the time, did he?"

Laura was speechless. This would certainly open up a whole range of new possibilities for her and Johnnie.

"I just hope you've remembered everything I taught you when we set sail

46

the other day. Now be off with you. She is all ship-shape and ready for a great voyage. Life is too short to be miserable."

"But what about you and your crew?" Laura asked.

"We'll be just fine. We managed fine before we ever set eyes on Nathaniel and we will again. He wasn't the easiest man in the world to work for, and quite frankly there's no love lost between him and the men. They didn't trust him, either, and it comes as no surprise to them that he's let them down. They're all going to enjoy the fun that we'll get from this situation," he said, his blue eyes twinkling with mischief.

Nathaniel had broken away from the group on the quayside for a moment and waved Laura over.

"You and the boy get on the ship and have the drinks and snacks organised for us as we come aboard," he ordered. "They should be finished with the photographs shortly."

Laura beckoned to Johnnie who was sitting alone on the harbour wall. Together they boarded *The Morada.*

"Oh! It's Nathaniel's lap dog," said Will sarcastically. He was still annoyed with her for putting up with the humiliation dished out by Nathaniel.

"Shut up!" she replied, "I just hope you're half as good a sailor as you make out."

Johnnie and Will exchanged glances but said nothing, sensing that there was something afoot.

"For the next ten minutes don't ask any questions, just do as I say, Johnnie, okay?"

Johnnie nodded, and Will looked on interestedly.

"Now Johnnie, when I give you the thumbs up, I want you to cut the ropes so that *The Morada* can move off. Will, it's your job to point those ropes out to him," she continued.

"Aye, aye, Captain," said Will, giving her a very smart salute. She rushed off down the galley steps, returning a few moments later with a very sharp carving knife.

"Use this," she said, handing it to Johnnie, "and pay no attention to anything Nathaniel might do or say."

Laura stood at the helm, took a deep breath, turned around and gave the signal to Will and Johnnie. Will showed Johnnie what to do and he cut frantically through the thick strands. Laura raised the anchor and started the engine. By the time Nathaniel realised what was happening, *The Morada* was already heading out of the harbour.

"What in God's name are you playing at, woman? Didn't you listen to a damned thing I said? I'll see you in jail for this, woman!" he yelled uncontrollably. Suddenly he realised that the crowd on the quayside had stopped chattering and were watching the little drama which was unfolding.

"This will all be sorted out in no time at all," he said to the waiting passengers, composing himself when he saw the looks of disbelief on their faces. "There may be a slight delay, but we'll set sail very shortly," he said.

They had paid good money to be the first set of passengers to sail on *The Morada's* maiden voyage and he didn't want them thinking they were going to have a wasted day.

"We have a mentally ill woman who has taken it upon herself to steal my ship, my good friends. The police and Coast Guard will apprehend this modern-day pirate and before you know it, you'll be setting sail as planned," he assured them.

The Coast Guard was in attendance at the launch and Nathaniel was instructing them to apprehend his wife, when a voice from behind him said, "I don't think you can arrest somebody for sailing their own ship, gentlemen, can you?"

Nathaniel turned around to see a very self-satisfied Gerry. "What the hell are you talking about?" he growled.

"I think you'll find that everything is in order, gentlemen," said Gerry, handing the Coast Guard the registration documents.

The coastguardsman examined the documents carefully. "And you say that the lady who has set sail is your wife?" he enquired.

"I'm sorry to say that she is," Nathaniel replied.

"Then everything does seem to be in order," he said, handing the forms to Nathaniel.

"No, that's not possible. I'm afraid there's been some kind of mistake…"

"No, sir, there's no mistake. Laura Banks is the legal owner of the vessel."

The Morada was no more than a speck on the horizon.

"Hey! Nathaniel!" Gerry shouted, "Who's going to be making the decisions now?" He saluted Nathaniel, and his crew roared with laughter as they headed homewards.

Aboard *The Morada* there was a stunned silence, as Johnnie and Will stood staring at Laura.

"Okay. You can ask questions now," she declared, laughing.

"Mum, what is going on?" shouted Johnnie, laughing hysterically.

"Thanks to Gerry, I'm the legal owner of The *Morada*," Laura told them. "He tricked Nathaniel into signing the ship over to me."

"Well I never! Cunning as an old fox," said Will, chuckling, "This is just the new start you and the boy needed, Laura."

"It's just the three of us now," said Johnnie. "We don't need anyone else."

Laura was glad to have got out of Nathaniel's clutches and Johnnie couldn't have looked happier, but she wondered what the future would hold for them.

"You've made the right decision, Laura, for both of you," Will said, with a reassuring smile.

"But what happens now, Will?" she replied anxiously.

"I'm a bit of an old fox myself you know," he chuckled. "I can feel it in me bones, Laura. We're gonna have many an adventure and many a tale to tell. Don't you worry about a thing. We're all gonna be just fine," Will said, looking steely-eyed and determined. There was a warmth and reassurance in Will's voice that made Johnnie and Laura feel safe and secure.

As they sailed off into a future of uncertainty, Will's thoughts turned once more to The Devil's Son.

CHAPTER FIVE
Myths and Legends

For the next hour of the voyage Will was noticeably quiet. Laura glanced at him and could see that he was deep in thought. "Are you okay, Will? I hope you're not regretting being landed with us," she said.

When he turned around there was a look of bewilderment on his face. "Not at all, you and the lad are the best thing that has happened to this old sea dog in a very long time. I'd never want either of you thinking I regretted a single minute. I just wish I could get rid of this dammed curse and be a real help to you and the lad," he said, shaking his head in disappointment.

"Will, if it wasn't for you our lives would have been unbearable and Johnnie and I would have drifted further and further apart," replied Laura. "You have been an absolute Godsend."

"Hold on a minute!" yelled Johnnie, startling Laura and Will with his outburst. "Every curse has a way of being lifted."

"Oh, you're right enough there, lad," said Will. "If a woman falls in love with me then the curse would be lifted, but I would die. Bit of a price to pay, don't you think?"

"Wait a minute, let me finish," said Johnnie. "In every book I have ever read the evil character who casts a spell or curses someone has a weakness. We *have* to find out more about The Devil's Son and his weaknesses," he stressed. "My old teacher used to say that knowledge is power. The more we know about The Devil's Son, the better the chance of finding ways to lift the curse."

There was a short silence as Laura and Will mulled over Johnnie's statement. Laura switched off the engine and dropped the anchor.

"Let's put our heads together and think about this," she said, scratching her head. "Can you think of *anything* in the yarns that the old sailors used to tell in the Inn that could help, Will?"

"Half the time I wasn't listening," he replied, staring out into the ocean. "I just thought it was the ravings of rum-filled old men." Will stared at the deck. "God, if only I knew," he said.

"The library!" said Johnnie. "We'll get all the books we can on myths and legends from the library. The legend of The Devil's Son is bound to be in one of them."

"Johnnie, I want to help Will, too, but we have to be practical. We need money to survive. We have absolutely nothing other than the shirts on our backs," said Laura.

"We've got two things of great value, folks," said Will, looking out to sea.

"What?" said Laura and Johnnie in unison.

"Friendship, and *The Morada*," replied Will. "Friendship is a thing no man can put a price on. And as for *The Morada*, we can use her as the pleasure boat she was going to be and make some money. There's food and drink in the galley. Plenty enough to go round."

"Yes!" shouted Johnnie. "That's it, Will! We'll make lots of money. Enough for a million books. I just knew you'd think of something."

"You always know the right thing to say," said Laura

Will lowered his head and looked slightly embarrassed. "Anyways," he said, changing the subject quickly, "we're going to have to think of a way to get folks to sail on this 'ere ship."

Laura looked skywards and realised that it wouldn't be long before darkness fell. "We can look at the map and berth *The Morada* in the nearest harbour," she said, looking deep in thought. "Then we can write out a sign informing people that there will be a cruise at mid day tomorrow."

"How much are we going to charge?" asked Johnnie.

Laura thought for a moment. "Twenty-five dollars each," she replied.

"What? Is that all?" said Johnnie

"We can't be greedy, Johnnie we're not giving people much notice. At this price word might get around because it's affordable," explained Laura.

"Yer mother's right, lad," said Will.

Johnnie nodded. "Okay, let's do it," he said.

Will and Laura checked the map and decided to berth *The Morada* at a place called Coral Cove. Johnnie wrote out a few signs and when they had dropped anchor for the night he went ashore and placed them strategically around the harbour. As night fell Laura could see that Johnnie was tired, so she took him down to the galley and sat with him until he fell asleep. When she returned, Will was standing at the helm of the ship, gazing up at the stars.

"A penny for your thoughts," she said, sneaking up behind him.

He jumped with fright and started to laugh. "I thought me heart was going to jump out me chest, woman," he said chortling.

"You know what amazes me about you, Will?" she said. "After everything that has happened in your life you still have your sense of humour, and you're so kind and thoughtful."

"Aye I'm wonderful now, but it's taken me two hundred years o' learnin'," he said with devilment in his eyes.

They laughed and chatted into the early hours of the morning.

"I'd better get off to bed," she said, stretching and yawning. "We have a long day ahead of us tomorrow. I haven't laughed so much in along time. Goodnight, Will."

"Aye, goodnight, Laura. Sleep well," said Will.

His eyes followed her as she left and then turned to gaze out into the ocean. It had been a very long time since he had laughed so much himself. He had always been a man who had enjoyed the company of women. It had been many years since his dear wife had passed away, but now she came into his mind. He'd often been away at sea for months on end, but what fun they'd had and how they'd laughed during his spells ashore. He realised he had missed that more than anything.

For several hours he stood gazing out into the ocean and did not even notice that the sun had risen on another perfect day. The sky was a clear blue by the time his train of thought was broken by Johnnie's shrieks of delight. "Wow! Check this out, Will!" he said. Will turned around to see queues of people on the quayside waiting to board the Morada.

"Well I never! Your mother was right again, lad," said Will, grinning from ear to ear. "You'd best go and waken her."

"Mum! Mum! Wake up!" he said, tugging at her sleeve.

"What is it, Johnnie? What's happened?" she said, still half asleep.

"Quickly, come up on deck!" said Johnnie clambering back upstairs.

Laura got out of her bunk and went up on deck. "What's going on?" she said.

"Take a look," said Will, pointing to the quayside.

"Oh my God!" she said, as she realised that the throng of people were *all* waiting to board. "What are we going to do? I just didn't expect so many. We'll never cope."

"Come along now, Laura. Don't be panickin'. It'll be fine," said Will calmly.

"The folks aren't stupid. They're not expecting a banquet for twenty-five dollars. They know a good deal when they see one."

Laura took a deep breath. "Okay, lets get this show on the road," she said, looking determined.

"Now that's more like the Laura I know," said Will, rubbing his hands in delight.

Laura headed off to make preparations, and by the time mid-day came she felt calm as she and Johnnie went onto the quayside to greet their very first guests. Johnnie collected the money and Laura welcomed them on board as if she had been doing it all her life.

Once all the passengers had boarded, Will could sense that Laura was nervous. "Come, Laura, you're the captain. Introduce yourself to these good people and tell them all you know of the history of *The Morada.* Everything will be fine," he assured her.

She smiled at Will and closed her eyes momentarily. *I can do this,* she thought.

Laura stood at the helm of the ship where everyone on board could see her. "Good afternoon, ladies and gentlemen," she said. "I am your captain, and I'd like to tell you a little bit about the history of the beautiful vessel on which you are going to sail today. Let me take you back two hundred years, to a time of pirates and vagabonds. *The Morada* belonged to a gentleman by the name of Captain William Joseph Francis. He was a decent man, but nevertheless a pirate. He was also a handsome man who was married,with two children, much to the annoyance of the ladies of the time, no doubt. Captain Will, as he was known, sailed the seven seas plundering riches from other ships. He was pursued for many years by Captain Maddock, one of the king's lawmen, but was never captured.

"*The Morada* was the fastest ship of her time. Captain Will and his crew set off one stormy night to capture a Spanish galleon, which was believed to be carrying a shipment of gold sovereigns. If successful, Captain Will and his crew had decided they would give up the pirate's life. Unfortunately the winds were against them and they headed back to Pearl Bay. Out of the darkness came *The Spawn,* a ship that, as legend would have us believe, was built by the Devil in the bowels of hell and was captained by his son. The Devil's Son and his crew murdered everyone on board *The Morada* with the exception of Captain Will. For showing contempt and no fear, The Devil's Son cursed Captain Will. As a ghost of sorts, he would now only be seen by people as tormented as himself. The curse would only be lifted if a woman fell in love with him, and then he would die.

"Captain Maddock discovered *The Morada,* buried the crew at sea, and then towed *The Morada* back to Pearl Bay. Legend has it that Captain Will walks the decks of *The Morada* to this day."

When she had finished, the ship's passengers were totally silent. It was an emotional moment. She was afraid to look in Will's direction for fear that he had been upset by the trip back in time. "Thank you Laura," said Will, his voice trembling. "I can't think of anyone I'd rather have telling Captain Will's story than you."

There was a lump in her throat, but she smiled at him and pulled herself together sufficiently to tell the passengers about the different stages of the restoration to the ship. After a round of applause from her spellbound audience, she raised the anchor, started the engine and *The Morada* turned out to sea.

Will stood at the helm beside Laura and watched Johnnie as he played happily with the children who were on board. Will realised that he had never seen him playing with other children. *The lad needs young uns around him more often.*

"Aye yer doin' a grand job," he said to Laura grinning.

"I would have given you a run for your money, Will," she laughed.

"Oh, I don't know about that, now," he chuckled.

"Is that because I'm a woman, Will?" said Laura.

"No, it's because I'm a man," he said, laughing heartily.

"Oh! Men," said Laura. "One day women will take over the world and men will only be allowed to do housework and shopping."

Will roared with laughter and Laura couldn't stop herself from joining in. Their laughter was interrupted by a woman's voice.

"I see what you're doing," she said, looking at Laura and grinning as if she knew something no one else did. "You're pretending you're having a conversation with that Captain Will, so we think he really is on the ship."

Laura couldn't answer the passenger as she was now laughing hysterically. The woman wandered off looking totally bemused. Laura and Will eventually composed themselves but did not even glance at each other for the rest of the voyage for fear of starting each other off again.

An hour or so later, Laura announced that she was going to drop the anchor, and that soft drinks and snacks would be served. She went to the galley, where she was joined by Johnnie and four other children. "Is it okay if my friends help us, Mum?" he said, with the widest grin.

"Of course it is," she replied, delighted that Johnnie had made some new friends so soon.

"I told you my mum would be okay about it," said Johnnie, placing the drinks and snacks onto trays. The children moved about the deck serving the passengers and Laura looked on proudly as Johnnie directed and organised them.

"A captain in the making he is, Laura," said Will.

"I think you might be right, Will," she said.

"I've an idea I'd like to put to you after the cruise," said Will, looking serious.

"That sounds a bit ominous," said Laura.

"It's just an idea. Don't be panickin' now," he said reassuringly.

I wonder what he has up his sleeve, she mused. Her train of thought was broken by a loud shriek. "Look over there! Look over there!" Laura turned around to see a child pointing out to the ocean. She joined the rest of the passengers who were looking over the side of the ship. A family of dolphins was performing for the passengers. Will and Johnnie clapped with delight as one of the dolphins leapt high out of the water and spun in the air before disappearing back into the deep blue water.

Laura turned the vessel around and was just about to begin the return leg of the journey when she noticed a man pointing into the clear blue waters. A small crowd had gathered round him and she strained to see what it was that they had noticed. The water was crystal clear, so clear, in fact, that she was amazed that they had not noticed the sunken vessel during their outward journey.

"I have heard rumours from old sailors in Coral Cove that *The Spawn* sank somewhere in these waters," he was saying. "What do you think, Captain? Do you think this sunken wreck could be *The Spawn?*" he called to Laura.

Within moments excited passengers were thronging around Laura to hear what she had to say on the subject.

"Is it really *The Spawn*, Captain?" asked one inquisitive little boy.

"Never in a million years is that the wreck of *The Spawn*," chuckled Will

"Well, young man, I couldn't really say for sure," said Laura, totally ignoring Will's observation, " but I've often found that there can be more than a grain of truth in the rumours of the old sailors from around these parts. I dare say we should not rule out the possibility that it could indeed be the wreck of *The Spawn*," she said, well aware that if this particular rumour took hold it would be no bad thing for the popularity of the cruises aboard *The Morada*.

Before long they were back in Coral Cove. The children on board had already convinced themselves that they had certainly seen the wreck of *The Spawn*. Laura knew that when they got home they would surely tell their friends about it. Next time she took *The Morada* past the spot, all she would have to do would be to refer to the rumour and before long it would be a permanent feature of the cruise.

"That was a bit of fancy footwork back there, Laura," chuckled Will, once the last of the passengers was safely ashore.

Laura laughed, "I didn't start the rumour," she said, but there's no sense in ruining folks' enjoyment if that's what they want to believe, now is there?

"Ah, you're quite the little businesswoman," said Will. "No reason why *The Spawn* shouldn't bring you a little luck."

They talked and laughed as they made their way back up the gangway. Johnnie ran excitedly ahead.

"Hurry up, Mum!" he shouted. "Let's see how much we've got."

"Hold your horses, Johnnie. It's been a long day," said Laura. "I'm going as fast as I can."

"This brings back a lot of memories," chuckled Will. "Countin' the fruits of yer labour after bein' out on the high seas."

Laura emptied the basket of collected money onto the table in the galley and started to count.

"How much have we got so far?" shouted Johnnie, who couldn't contain himself any longer.

"Shh! You'll make me lose count," said Laura.

Eventually she placed the last dollar bill on the table and stared at the pile of money. There was a long, drawn out silence. Johnnie thought he was going to burst with anticipation.

"How much, Mum?" he said anxiously.

"Including tips, we have the grand sum of five hundred and fifty dollars," declared Laura.

"Wow!" exclaimed Johnnie, "we're rich."

"I wouldn't go as far as that," chuckled Laura.

"Just imagine the books we could buy with five hundred dollars, Will," said Johnnie.

"Me thinks there's more important things to be done, lad," replied Will.

"What could be more important than finding out a way to rid you of the curse, Will?" asked Laura.

"You and the lad need to be settled," said Will. "A home and friends - somewhere to belong to. You can 'ave all that here in Coral Bay. And by using *The Morada* as a pleasure boat you could make a king's ransom 'n all."

"That was the only reason we did the cruise in the first place, Will. So that we could find a way of lifting the curse," said Johnnie.

"Aye, yer right, lad, and I'm honoured that you and your mother want to help me, but I've had me time," replied Will.

Johnnie stood up and ran to the galley stairs. "You don't care about us. You're just scared that The Devil's Son will beat you again," he yelled, as he scrambled upstairs and onto the deck.

Embarrassed, and angry with Johnnie, Laura made to go after him.

"It's me the lad's angry with," said Will, "Would you be mindin' if I goes up and talks to him meself?"

Laura agreed, and Will arrived on deck to find Johnnie slumped over the side of the ship staring into the distance.

"Sovereign for your thoughts," said Will.

"How stupid are you?" snarled Johnnie. "It's a penny for your thoughts."

Will looked skyward. *This ain't gonna be easy.* "Look lad, I know you're angry, but…"

"I don't want to talk to you," screamed Johnnie, interrupting Will. "We could have been a family, but you're not interested."

"Johnnie, there's nothin' that would 'ave made me prouder than to 'ave you and your mother as family," replied Will.

"Then why don't we go after The Devil's Son and try to lift the curse?" Johnnie pleaded, his eyes welling with tears.

Will leaned over the side of the ship beside him.

"I've wandered around this world for two hundred years, lad, and it just ain't natural," he said. "I should 'ave passed away and been with my family, nearly two centuries ago. I don't want to think about The Devil's Son anymore. I've thought of nothing else since that horrible night, and dined on hate, bitterness and revenge for far too long. We are put on this earth to make the best of what we have. If things don't go according to plan we should still be grateful at being given the gift of life, and make the most of it. I 'ave 'ad me life and realise that it wasn't that bad at all. If we went after The Devil's Son and somethin' happened to you or your mother it would be a victory for evil and even more heartache for me, and I'm not about to let that happen. I realise now that I won't ever truly be at rest, till I meet me maker, crew and loved ones. I'm sorry lad, if you don't understand that, but it's how I feel."

There was an uneasy silence, which was broken by Laura. "Have you two made up yet?" she shouted from the galley.

"Well lad? 'Ave we?" said Will, looking at Johnnie.

He nodded. "Sorry, Will," he said quietly.

"No need for sorry, lad," said Will. "We should spit on our palms now and shake 'ands to seal the friendship. But old Will can't do that anymore."

"Yuck! That's gross," shrieked Johnnie, covering his face with his hands.

By the time Johnnie and Will joined Laura in the galley, wonderful smells of supper cooking were wafting through the air.

"Is everything sorted out then?" she asked.

"Everythin' is just dandy," replied Will. Johnnie smiled and nodded in agreement.

They spent the rest of the evening discussing the events of the day. Johnnie enthused about the new friends he had made on the cruise and how they lived and went to school in Coral Cove. He now had friends to meet up with. It was a unanimous decision; all things considered, it had been a good day.

CHAPTER SIX
Testing Times

Early the next morning Laura awoke but there was no sign of Will. She searched *The Morada* from top to bottom but he was nowhere to be found. Suddenly there was a shout from behind her. "Ahoy there, Capt'n."

Laura spun round to find Will grinning from ear to ear. "Where have *you* been? I didn't know what to think," she said.

"I was looking for a dwelling for you 'n the lad," replied Will, looking pleased with himself.

"Could you just let me know before you wander off like that?" she asked sharply.

"Come on, smile for Will. It's too nice a day to be cross wi' me," he teased.

Shrugging her shoulders, Laura gave him a grand smile.

"Will, what do you mean you were looking for a dwelling?" she asked.

"You 'n the lad don't want to be living on *The Morada* forever now, do you? Once folks spread the word about the cruises, you'll have enough money to buy a dwelling fit for a king, or a queen," he said.

"But what about the books and The Devil's Son?" said Laura.

"That can wait," said Will. "You 'n' the lad needs to be settled. Johnnie needs friends and schoolin'."

"But Johnnie is *desperate* to help you and so am I. You've done so much for us," she said.

"The lad will be fine. He'll understand. And you're to be thinkin' about him first, not old Will," he said.

The conversation ended there as Johnnie appeared from the galley.

"Mornin' lad. And how are you this very fine day?" said Will.

"Fine, thanks, Will," replied Johnnie, yawning.

"How do you fancy taking a walk into town and getting some new clothes, Johnnie?" said Laura.

"Can we afford it, Mum?" asked Johnnie.

"Yes, we can, and even if we couldn't afford it, you can't walk around looking like Jim Hawkins forever," she replied.

"Johnnie looks nothin' like Jim Hawkins. He was taller and…"

"It was a joke, Will," said Laura interrupting.

Johnnie and Laura laughed as Will tried to work out what was so funny.

"How do you fancy settling in Coral Cove for a while Johnnie?" asked Laura.

He thought for a moment. "If it's okay with you and Will, it's okay with me," he replied, winking at Will.

"Right, then. That is settled," declared Laura. "We'll get some supplies in town and some new clothes. Then we'll think about some sort of advertising campaign for the cruises."

"You'll 'ave to be careful in town, mind you," stressed Will. "There be all sorts of weird lookin' vessels scurryin' round the place. They be fast 'n all."

Johnnie and Laura laughed, realising that Will was referring to the modes of transport he'd seen.

The town was small but it had enough shops to give Laura and Johnnie a reasonable choice of clothes. The noise of the vehicles and the hustle and bustle of people coming and going amazed Will. Laura and Johnnie were convinced that if he shook his head in disbelief any more, it would fall off. When they had completed their purchases, they arranged for everything to be delivered that afternoon to *The Morada*, and they were then free to go with Will to see the house he had found for them earlier that morning. They stood gazing in awe at the sprawling place with its manicured gardens and swimming pool.

"What do you think folks?" he asked.

"Wow, it's awesome!" enthused Johnnie. "I could play football there all day, then dive into the pool to cool down."

"The price will be awesome too," said Laura. "But I suppose dreaming doesn't cost a penny."

"Once *The Morada* starts payin' her way you could buy the town," chuckled Will.

"We're allowed to dream, Will. No one can take that from us," said Laura.

"We never know what life has in store for us, Laura," said Will sagely.

They arrived back at *The Morada* to find a large, well-dressed man with a big white beard scribbling on a pad at the foot of the gangway.

"Can I help you?" Laura enquired.

"Oh, good afternoon," replied the man. "I'm Harold Winters, the harbour master."

"You're English," said Johnnie excitedly.

"I am," he replied. "I hail from Manchester, originally, but I have lived here for more years than I care to remember."

"Is everything okay, Mr. Winters?" quizzed Laura.

"Yes, just the usual formalities, Miss. And please, call me Harry," he replied. "I had a day's holiday yesterday or I could have tied this up already."

"Formalities? What formalities?" Laura asked.

"Could I see your nautical license and registration papers?"

Laura's heart sank. She had the registration documents but no nautical license.

"I don't have a nautical licence," she replied.

. "Oh dear," replied Harry. "I'm afraid the ship won't be able to leave the harbour with you at the wheel then, Miss."

Johnnie and Will couldn't believe what they were hearing.

"Is there any way I can apply for a license?" asked Laura.

"Certainly, I'll drop an application form in to you later today. Complete that and you will be sent confirmation of a test date," he replied.

"Test date? Do I have to sit a test?" she asked.

"Yes, indeed. We send you out a test date and on that day you sit a theory test and a practical examination," he said.

Laura held her head in her hands. "How long will it take between applying and sitting the test?" she asked anxiously.

"Oh, about a week or two," Harry replied.

"A week or two!" gasped Johnnie.

"Harry, without going into details, Johnnie and I have been through enough. We just want to be settled in Coral Cove so I really need the license quickly so that we can make a living," said Laura.

"I see. Leave it with me," he said, before driving off in his car.

There was a stunned silence as Laura, Johnnie and Will tried to take in what had just happened.

"Cheer up, folks, we're not done for yet. It's just a matter o' time. Nothin' that's worthwhile is ever easy," said Will, trying to cheer them up.

"But I'm going to have to sit a test, Will. It's years since I had to sit a test," said Laura.

"Have faith in yourself Laura. Everythin' will be just fine," said Will.

"I wish I shared your optimism," said Laura, her voice tinged with anxiety.

"Mum, it doesn't matter how many times you fail, just keep trying," said Johnnie. "Will and I will help you."

Will winced and covered his face with his hands.

"No doubt about it Johnnie, you are definitely a man in the making," said Laura, chuckling.

Some time later, just as they had finished storing the supplies away, the noise of a car horn disturbed the peaceful afternoon. From the deck they watched as Harry, armed with a pile of books, made his way up the gangway. "Hi, folks! Good news and bad news," he said, handing the books to Laura.

"I think we'll have the good news first," said Laura.

"If you fill in the forms we will process them right away and get you logged on to the computer records," he said.

"And the bad news?" replied Laura, dreading Harry's reply.

"The waiting time is four weeks for the test but…"

"Four weeks?" said Laura, interrupting.

"Yes, but there's been a cancelation. Unfortunately it's tomorrow at two p.m."

"Yes!" exclaimed Johnnie. "You can do it, Mum!"

"Tomorrow!" gasped Laura. "I'll never be able to read all those books by tomorrow."

"It's the best I could do in the circumstances," said Harry. "I've written down the main questions you'll be asked and referenced them to the books you need to consult."

"Thanks, Harry, I do appreciate you going out of your away for us," Laura replied. "It's just so much to try and take in with the time I have."

"I don't mean to add to the burden," he replied, "but there is also a charge of ninety dollars for the test."

"It just gets better," said Laura sarcastically.

"Come on, where's that feisty lady who never gives up?" shouted Will.

Laura took a deep breath. "Okay, I'll take the test," she said.

Johnnie jumped up on Laura and hugged her. "You can do it, Mum. I know you can do it," he said, squeezing her tight.

"You'll have us both in the water, if you don't get down," she said, chuckling.

"I'll inform the examiner to be here for two p.m. He'll complete the theory test aboard the ship, then he will take you out to sea for the practical part of the examination," said Harry.

"Thanks for everything, Harry," she said. "You've really gone out of your way to help us and you didn't need to."

"I've a daughter back in England and a grandson I've never seen," said Harry. "I just hope if they were ever in need, someone would try to help them. Anyway, good luck for tomorrow," he said as he walked down the gangway, jumped into his car and drove off.

"Well, I think we all know what I'll be doing tonight," said Laura. "You two can cook supper. I've got studying to do."

Later on that evening, when supper was cleared away, Johnnie and Will asked questions from the books and Laura attempted to answer. She was getting more and more frustrated at the amount of questions she was failing to answer.

"This just isn't going to work. There's just not enough time," she groaned.

"Calm down. Laura, yer doin' just fine," said Will.

"Doing fine? I've only answered two questions correctly so far, Will," she replied.

"Clear yer mind, and concentrate on the books, " said Will.

Laura and Will continued to go over the questions long after Johnnie had gone to bed.

"If I fail the test it will be weeks before I get another chance," said Laura anxiously. "And once I've paid the test fee we're left with about ten dollars. How will we survive?"

"All you can do is try yer best, Laura. There be enough supplies for you 'n' the lad, so don't be panickin' about that. If you don't pull it off tomorrow then we'll keep tryin' until you do," said Will, reassuringly.

.   When Johnnie awoke the next morning, Laura and Will were still poring over the books.

"Mum, you'd better get some sleep, or you won't be ready for the test," said Johnnie.

"The lad's spot on, Laura," agreed Will.

"I suppose you're right," yawned Laura, heading down the galley stairs.

"What do you think, Will, has she got a chance?" Johnnie asked, tentatively.

"It's a hard task, lad. But yer mother is a fine strong-willed woman and if there's anyone that can do it, she can," replied Will.

"I hope so, Will. She has worked hard and I know she'll be upset if she fails," said Johnnie.

A couple of hours later a car pulled up alongside *The Morada*. "You'd better waken yer mother, lad. I think it's time," said Will anxiously.

Laura felt that she had just rested her head on the pillow when a slightly nervous Johnnie awakened her.

"Mum, the man's here for the test," he said in a whisper.

"What, already?" she groaned.

Calmly, she rose, slipped into her clothes and made her way on deck.

A stony-faced man with greased-back black hair and thick-rimmed spectacles was checking around *The Morada*.

"Everything seems to be in order," he said, looking slightly disappointed that this was the case.

"What happens now?" asked Laura.

"First of all, the boy will have to leave the ship," he insisted.

"But why?" Laura asked.

"Section one, paragraph three of the Coral Cove nautical manual states, 'Only the subject of the test and the Examiner will be present for the duration of the nautical examination.'" he quoted.

"Okay, I'll go," said Johnnie, heading down the gangway in a huff.

"I'll take the lad into town Laura. Just you clear yer mind," said Will.

Johnnie and Will watched from the shore as Laura sat down and started the test.

"Come on, lad. Us watchin' yer mother might spook her," said Will.

They headed into town and stood at the gates of the sprawling mansion that they had visited the day before. "One day you and yer mother will live in this house. You mark my words, lad, " said Will.

Not a word was spoken as they turned and headed back into town. The silence was broken when a car backfired and Will leapt high into the air with fright. Johnnie laughed so much at Will's reaction that his ribs began to ache.

"Oh, the big brave pirate!" laughed Johnnie, mocking Will.

"I was just checking if there were cannons high up on those buildings, so I could protect you, lad," exclaimed an embarrassed Will.

"Sure, Will," chortled Johnnie.

"You've got to 'ave you're wits about you at all times, lad. Landlubbers are always worth the watchin'," said Will, trying to give credibility to his actions.

After an hour or so they headed back to the harbour.

As they approached *The Morada* the examiner walked down the gangway.

"How did Mum get on?" asked Johnnie, excitedly.

"It is the responsibility of the subject of the examination to pass on that information, not the examiner," he replied, walking past them.

Johnnie screwed up his face and, walking behind the examiner, mouthed what he had just said and mimicked his unusual walk.

"I fear the worst lad," said Will.

"We have to let her know that it doesn't matter if she failed," whispered Johnnie.

"Aye, yer right lad," replied Will.

They boarded *The Morada* to find Laura slumped over the ship's wheel.

"Mum it doesn't matter," said Johnnie reassuringly. "We'll be okay."

"That scurvy dog wouldn't know a sailor from a swamp rat," growled Will.

Laura straightened herself up and, looking more than pleased with herself, handed an official-looking piece of paper to Johnnie. After a minute of perusing the text he slowly lifted his head. "You passed," he said. "Will, Mum passed!"

"Well I'll be darned," said Will. "If I could, I'd 'ave a tot o' rum in yer honour."

"Sleeping is the only way I'd like to celebrate," said Laura, yawning.

"You go and 'ave your sleep, and me and the lad will tend to things," said Will.

Will organised and planned what tasks needed to be completed for the cruises and Johnnie carried out his directions. The departure times were advertised on the chalkboard along with the price of twenty-five dollars per person. Shopkeepers in town were informed of the cruise times and prices so they could alert both the locals and tourists on the island. By the time the tasks had been completed and Johnnie had eaten, he was absolutely worn out.

"You be gettin' off to bed now, lad. You've worked hard," said Will.

"Okay, Will, I'll see you in the morning," replied Johnnie, barely able to keep his eyes open.

A short while later Laura appeared back on deck.

"Well, if it ain't Captain Laura herself," said Will smiling.

"Not quite a captain yet, Will, but it's a start," she replied.

"Well in my eyes, you're Captain Laura," said Will saluting.

Laura smiled, leaned on the side of the ship and gazed out into the ocean.

"What a year this has been. Johnnie and I were almost out on the street; I got married to a tyrant, moved to a new country, met a ghost, obtained a ship and became a sailor," she said, chuckling in disbelief.

"Aye, but now you 'n' the lad are happy," purred Will. "Everythin' is for a reason."

"Everything changed for the better when we met you, Will. You've brought out strength in me I never knew existed. And Johnnie has learned so much from you," she replied, her voice quivering with emotion.

"Now don't you be gettin' all sentimental on me," replied Will. "You always 'ad strength; it took a lot o' guts to come through what you 'ave."

"You know everything there is to know about Johnnie and me, but apart from the curse all I know is that you had a wife and two daughters," said Laura.

There was an awkward silence.

"I'm sorry," she said. "I can't believe how stupid I can be sometimes. It must be too painful to talk about. Forget I mentioned it."

"No, it's fine, Laura. I just 'aven't spoken about them as real folks in a long, long time," said Will, softly. He sighed and continued, "My wife's name was Louisa. She was small, fair-haired and had eyes as green as emeralds. She also had a fiery temper, when riled. But she was loving, kind and a good wife and mother. How she put up wi' me I'll never know.

"Me youngest daughter was Isabella. She was only six, but already had her mother's looks and temper to match. I'd pity any man who'd try to make a fool o' her. Beth was me eldest. Twelve she was. Always cleanin' and scrubbin' somethin' she was. Always wantin' to help other folks. She was her father's girl. Louisa told me that every night I was at sea, Beth would say a prayer for me, then open the door and blow a kiss towards the sea. I was a lucky man, and know that even more now, as I look back."

Will looked at Laura, smiled and said, "I never thought I'd be able to talk about them again without hollerin' and blubberin', but it feels good, Laura. Thanks."

Laura and Will whiled away the rest of the evening reminiscing about their first meeting and the events that had taken place during the restoration of *The Morada*. Then they debated and discussed life in general. Will came to the conclusion that life was a series of tests but with no pass marks. Laura agreed with Will's philosophy but reckoned her tests had been marked, in the form of wrinkles. He argued that he thought they must be fine grades then, as they had only added to her beauty.

CHAPTER SEVEN
Festive Spirit

At the end of the long summer holiday, Johnnie started at his new school. It was a small island school and only very rarely did new children come to it. Most of the children who went to Crystal Cove School had lived on the island all their lives, as had their parents and grandparents. Some had visited the mainland but many had never ventured off the island in their lives. Johnnie very quickly became popular with the island children. They loved his English accent and the stories he would tell of his life in England. It was so different from the tropical paradise that was all they had ever known.

Johnnie was an independent youngster, who had spent a great deal of time in adult company. He was talkative and sociable and taught them lots of new songs and riddles from home. *The Morada*, which had now become their home, resounded with the laughter of the many friends who would call on him. They taught him how to fish and he spent many happy hours with them, shrimping or hunting for crabs in the rocky pools of the island's beautiful beaches. At home in England Johnnie and his friends had loved nothing better than a good game of football after school. They also played for the school team and enjoyed playing against different schools in the area.

Johnnie thought that when he moved to America the children would probably only play American football, baseball or basketball; he didn't realize that there were professional football teams in America as well. So he was in his element when he discovered that the children at his new school loved to play soccer, as they called it, and that they also had a school team. Johnnie was desperate to play for the school team but was nervous about going to the practice session in case he just wasn't good enough. He plucked up the courage to attend and although he was nervous to begin with, it wasn't long before he was scoring goals and receiving high fives from his impressed classmates. At the end of one practice session Mr. Bradley came in to the games hall with a list of names and began announcing the pool of players who would be representing Coral Cove School for the forthcoming fixtures. Johnnie sat with his head in his hands for what seemed like an eternity, praying that his name would be read out. At last it came. "Johnnie Jackson," said Mr. Bradley, smiling. His new teammates surrounded him and again it was high fives all round. Johnnie beamed with contentment. At last he truly felt he belonged on the island.

Encouraged by his new friends he was soon trying out baseball, American football and basketball. Before long he was attending practices in all of these sports and had a hectic schedule. But he loved every minute of his new life. He still managed to find some time to help out on *The Morada* and loved nothing better at the end of the day than to regale Will with stories of how his day had been. Laura and Will noticed that the pale, sad little boy they had known had vanished, and he now looked as sun-kissed and healthy as the island children.

The Morada was doing rather well. The cruises had steadily become immensely popular and Laura was building a good reputation of value for money and good service. In a very short space of time, *The Morada* had become an attraction of Coral Cove and curious tourists were flocking to take photographs and sail on the mysterious vessel. Local businesses were also cashing in on *The Morada's* popularity and were selling t-shirts and all sorts of gifts and memorabilia relating to the mysterious ship. Laura was making a good living. Finances could not yet run to the sprawling house with the manicured gardens and swimming pool that Will had found for them, but they were all happy and that was all that mattered.

Christmas was fast approaching and this now became the focus of Laura's attention. She was determined to make it a Christmas to remember for Johnnie and Will, one that they could look back on for years to come. With Johnnie's help, she decked out *The Morada* from top to bottom with Christmas lights. She bought a musical Santa Claus that danced and sang. Will spent hours watching in amazement as the hilarious little figure went through his routine, again and again. Laura found his child-like fascination with the toy both touching and intriguing.

Laura switched on the Christmas lights as Johnnie and Will looked on.

"Wow!" exclaimed Johnnie, "They're cool. What do you think, Will?"

"Aye lad, they're cool," chuckled Will.

"What would you like for Christmas, lad?" quizzed Will.

"A Rolling Stones CD," said Johnnie, laughing.

"The Rolling Stones?" spluttered Laura. "Where have you heard The Rolling Stones?"

"At my friend Frankie's house. His dad plays them all the time," Johnnie replied. "They're cool."

"Can't you listen to Westlife or Boyzone like any normal child your age?" replied Laura.

"What? You can't be serious. They are so yesterday," said Johnnie.

"Has an American alien taken over your body and started working your vocal chords?" said Laura. "And anyway, The Rolling Stones were around in the sixties, so how yesterday is that?"

"I give up; you can be so un-cool at times, Mum," said Johnnie shaking his head disapprovingly, as he headed down the galley stairs.

"What in God's name was that all about?" asked Will, looking totally bewildered.

"Absolutely nothing," laughed Laura. "Absolutely nothing."

As Christmas approached, Johnnie became more and more excited and talked incessantly. Will threatened to throw him overboard on a number of occasions if he continued, and Laura had promised that she would help.

On the evening of his school play, things had gone to the other extreme; after days of non-stop talking he was unusually silent. Laura and Will were glad of the respite but soon realised that there was something troubling him.

"Are you alright, lad?" Will asked.

Johnnie nodded but there was no reply.

"Are you sure, lad?" inquired Will.

Johnnie nodded his head, but still there was no answer.

"Are you nervous about appearing in the play tonight, Johnnie?" Laura enquired gently.

Again there was no reply.

"You go out there, Johnnie, and do the best that you can. That's all I expect from you," said Laura. "If things don't go according to plan, then so be it. I'm so proud of you for trying."

"Yer mother's right, lad," said Will. "You can only give it yer best shot. That's all there is to it."

"But what if I forget my lines or trip on the stage or something? Everybody will laugh at me," said Johnnie. "We're performing *Oliver* and I'm the only real English person in the play."

"Everyone in the play is in the same situation, Johnnie. Sometimes in life you have to take a chance that things will work out okay," said Laura, trying to reassure him.

"Yer mothers right, lad. We all 'ave to face our demons at one time or another," said Will.

After a long silence Johnnie stood up. "Right. Let's go," he said, "I'll give it my best shot."

"Now that's more like it, lad," said Will. "You're yer mother's son right enough."

When they arrived at the school hall it was full of nervous parents, grandparents, aunts, uncles and cousins. There were no more seats available so Laura and Will took up a position against the back wall. An extremely nervous Johnnie trooped off with the rest of the cast to prepare. Before he disappeared backstage he gave Laura and Will a little wave. They too were beginning to pick up on the atmosphere of tension tinged with excitement in the audience. *Please, please, don't let him fluff his lines or miss a cue*, thought Laura.

"The lad will be just fine, Laura, mark me words," Will reassured her.

"Oh, I hope so, Will; my stomach is in knots," Laura replied nervously, receiving a few strange glances from people who were unaware of Will's presence, and therefore witnessed her talking to herself. The curtain was raised and Will shouted and whistled his appreciation as Johnnie made his appearance. Laura could feel her throat drying up.

"Ladies and gentlemen, welcome to Coral Cove School. My name is The Artful Dodger," said Johnnie, bowing to the audience. "I hope you will enjoy our production of *Oliver,* which was written by Charles Dickens." He left the stage with applause ringing in his ears.

Yes! I did it! I did it, thought Johnnie.

Laura was so proud she could have wept. Will continued to clap and shout long after Johnnie had left the stage. This set the scene for the whole evening. At the end of the play Johnnie made his way back to be with Laura and Will.

"Well done, Johnnie," said Laura, beaming with pride.

"I don't need to ask you what you thought, Will. I heard you shouting all the way through the show," chuckled Johnnie.

"Just lettin' you know I was behind you, lad," replied Will, smiling.

They headed back to *The Morada,* where Will re-enacted the whole play, much to the amusement of Johnnie and Laura. After supper, Laura tucked Johnnie into bed and joined Will on deck.

"Now, that was a good evening," she said.

"The lad was a credit to you, Laura," replied Will.

"He was a credit to *us*," Laura said. "I don't know how I would have coped without you."

There was a short silence.

"We'll just 'ave to accept it Laura," replied Will.

"Accept what?" said Laura.

"That I'm wonderful," chuckled Will.

"You are absolutely impossible, Will Francis," said Laura, laughing.

"I mean it Laura, Johnnie's a fine lad and he'll make you proud of him," said Will.

"I hope you're right, Will. You just never know what's ahead of you," said Laura.

"It's not often old Will's wrong. Is it now?" he chuckled.

"I don't want to make you even more big-headed by admitting to that, but so far you've had a pretty good track record," chuckled Laura.

It was quite late when Laura went off to bed that night. She should have been tired but somehow sleep escaped her. Her thoughts were of Will and how things might have been. When she finally fell asleep just before daylight she dreamt that Will had died and she awoke with a start. The next morning she was unusually quiet after Johnnie had gone off to school. She helped the crew to prepare for the midday cruise as usual, but Will could sense that all was not well.

"Cat got yer tongue this mornin', Laura?" he said, smiling.

"I can't be sweetness and light every day," she replied. "I'm busy, I have a business to run."

Will was utterly bewildered. He had never seen her like this before. He leaned over the side of the ship, staring out over the water lost in his thoughts. The midday cruise went well, but Laura hadn't spoken to him during the entire trip.

When Johnnie arrived back from school he was jubilant. He was now officially on holiday. "Ye ha!" he exclaimed, "no more school!"

"Well, that may be so," said Laura. "But there's plenty to be done around here. We have to get ready for the Christmas Eve cruise."

"Are you okay, Mum?" said Johnnie, surprised at Laura's reaction.

"Why is everybody so concerned about me all of a sudden?" Laura replied, scurrying down to the galley.

Johnnie glanced over to Will, who was staring out into the ocean.

" What's going on, Will?" he asked.

" I don't know, lad," replied Will, shrugging his shoulders.

There was quietness aboard *The Morada* that Johnnie had only ever known when Nathaniel had been around. When it was time for dinner Will stayed on deck and Johnnie joined his mother in the galley.

Johnnie couldn't stand the silence any longer.

"Mum, what's going on? What's wrong?" he asked.

" Eat up, Johnnie. There is nothing wrong," Laura insisted.

"But…"

"Johnnie!! No more!!" exclaimed Laura, interrupting.

They ate the rest of the meal in an awkward silence. Johnnie washed up the dishes and went up on deck to be with Will.

"I think Mum's just tired, Will," said Johnnie. "She'll be alright later."

"Aye lad, she's probably just tired," replied Will. "Yer mother's been workin' hard. And I'm not much help."

"Yes you are, Will. You keep Mum happy," said Johnnie. "That's the most important job."

"You're old beyond yer years, lad," said Will.

Laura didn't appear from the galley all evening. Johnnie tried to persuade her to join them on deck, but she still seemed distracted and deep in her own thoughts.

" I'm too tired, Johnnie," she said.

By the time Johnnie had said goodnight to Will and clambered down the galley stairs, Laura was already in bed.

"Goodnight, Mum," he said, climbing into his bed. "I hope you feel better tomorrow."

"Goodnight, Johnnie," she replied.

She felt bad about not spending any time with him but she was confused. Her mind was still racing over her sleepless night and her unsettling dream about Will. She spent another restless night wrestling with her thoughts until eventually, exhausted, she dropped off to sleep.

Next morning, she was up bright and early. She prepared breakfast and wakened Johnnie.

"Up you get, sleepy head! Your breakfast is on the table," she said.

Johnnie slipped into his clothes, ate breakfast and washed the dishes.

"I'm going on deck to see Will, Mum," he said.

A few moments later he came scrambling back down the galley stairs.

"He's gone. Will's gone," he said, pacing up and down. "Hurry up and get ready, Mum, we have to go and find him."

Laura stood up and started clearing the table.

"Maybe it's for the best, Johnnie," she said.

Johnnie was so angry he could hardly get the words out.

"What?" he spluttered. "What do you mean, maybe it's for the best?"

"Maybe Will thought it was time to move on and help someone else," she said, wiping down the table.

"He wouldn't just leave *The Morada*. It's his home," said Johnnie, unable to work out his mother's reasoning.

There was a short silence.

"Not unless he was made to feel unwelcome," he stated.

There was no reply from Laura.

"You have said or done something to make him feel as if he wasn't wanted, haven't you?" roared Johnnie, scrambling back up the galley stairs.

Laura followed Johnnie up the stairs and onto the deck. He was halfway down the gangway.

"You don't understand, Johnnie," she shouted.

Johnnie stopped in his tracks, turned around and with venom in his voice shouted,

"Oh, I understand now. No wonder my dad left. I hate you!" before disappearing into town.

A few hours later, looking rather crestfallen, he returned without Will

He made his way below deck, totally ignoring his mother. By the time Laura joined him in the galley, he was already undressed and in bed.

"Johnnie, you've got to believe…"

"Go away. I don't want to speak to you!" he shouted.

Back on deck, she sat alone, distraught and confused, wrestling with her thoughts. *Well done. You've just got him back and now you've lost him again*. Will had only been gone for a few hours, but she missed him already.

The next morning, Laura awoke but Johnnie was nowhere to be found. She quickly dressed and rushed into town. No one had seen him. She walked around to the far end of the harbour and spied him sitting on the rocks. He was a sad and lonely little figure.

Laura walked slowly over and sat down on the rocks beside him.

"Johnnie, I didn't mean to hurt you or Will, but…"

"Is Will back yet?" he scowled, interrupting her.

"No, he's not," she replied, lowering her head.

He stood up and walked back along the rocks towards *The Morada*. She followed behind, not knowing what to do or say. The crew had already started arriving to prepare for the midday cruise.

"Whatever you think of me, Johnnie, we still have a business to run," said Laura.

"You wouldn't have a business if we hadn't met Will," replied Johnnie and walked off to help the crew.

Laura felt lower than she had in a very long time. She put on a brave face to greet the cruise guests and went through the motions until the last passenger had disembarked. She was not looking forward to the remainder of the day. Johnnie decided that he was going ashore to play with some of his friends, so Laura headed into town for some last minute shopping and some more decorations for the Christmas Eve cruise. As she walked around the shops her thoughts turned to happier times...The conversations she and Will used to have in the evenings. The laughs they shared during the restoration of *The Morada*. And the way Will could make her feel better with a few wise words.

Back at *The Morada*, Johnnie, who was still in a foul mood, joined her as she walked up the gangplank.

"Did you have a nice time?" she said, trying to make conversation, "Would you like something to eat?"

Ignoring her completely, he stomped off downstairs and she followed him into the galley.

"Johnnie, we have got to talk about this," she said, reaching out her hand to him. He pushed her hand aside.

"I'm not ready to talk about anything!" he shouted. "Just leave me alone."

"Okay, Johnnie. But I'm not going anywhere," she replied. "I'm here when you're ready to talk."

She occupied herself for the rest of the evening by putting the finishing touches to the Christmas decorations and checking that everything was in place for the Christmas Eve cruise.

The next morning, Laura awoke dreading the day ahead. Christmas had lost all meaning. Johnnie hated her and Will would not be around to make her laugh. *Well I got what I wished for, a Christmas to remember*, she thought. She decided to pull herself together and try to get into the spirit of things.

"Good morning, Johnnie. Not long 'till Christmas now. Are you excited yet?" said Laura, trying to exude enthusiasm.

"Ecstatic," Johnnie replied sarcastically.

"I wonder what Santa Clause will bring you?" Laura asked, chuckling.

"Hopefully a mum who doesn't get rid of people I love," replied Johnnie scathingly.

Laura felt as if her heart had been ripped out and thrown on the floor.

"I'm meeting my friends in town," said Johnnie, climbing the galley stairs.

He met his friends, but somehow he couldn't enjoy himself. He was angry with his mum, but he felt bad about what he had said to her. He knew that he'd hurt her deeply. He was sorry, but he just felt so confused. He had so many questions to ask. He needed to know why his dad had left them all those years ago and why his mum had married Nathaniel. And he just couldn't get Will out of his mind. *What had she said or done to make him leave so abruptly, just when everything seemed to be going so well?* He made up his mind that when he returned to *The Morada* he would get the truth from his mother. Even if the truth hurt, he was determined that he wasn't going to be confused anymore.

A few hours later he returned to find Laura showing a smartly dressed man around *The Morada.*

"Hi, Johnnie. This is Mr. D'Angelo," said Laura, hoping Johnnie would be civil.

"Pleased to meet you," said Johnnie.

"Likewise," said Mr. D'Angelo.

"If you can occupy yourself just now Johnnie… I will be with you shortly," said Laura, hoping that he wouldn't make a scene.

Johnnie had no idea who the man was, but knew he must be important, as his mum was speaking in her poshest accent. Almost an hour later Mr. D'Angelo left.

"Who was that, Mum?" he asked.

"That, Johnnie, was Mr. D'Angelo from D'Angelo Entertainments in New York," said Laura.

"New York!" exclaimed Johnnie. "What did he want?"

"One of his employees had been on one of our cruises and loved it," replied Laura. "He returned to work and spoke to Mr. D'Angelo about *The Morada.* So, he decided to fly down and have a look for himself."

"He came all the way from New York to cruise on our ship?" exclaimed Johnnie.

"No, he came all the way from New York to make us a business proposal," replied Laura.

"What sort of proposal?" he said anxiously, fearing that Mr. D'Angelo wanted to buy *The Morada*.

"He wants to rent *The Morada* from us for six months of every year," she replied. "He wants to take *The Morada* round the shores of America."

"But where would we live?" asked Johnnie.

"We can't live on *The Morada* forever, Johnnie. We always knew we would have to buy a house," replied Laura. "And two hundred and fifty thousand dollars a year may just help us to achieve that."

Johnnie's eyes nearly popped out of their sockets. "Two hundred and fifty thousand dollars," he spluttered, "And *The Morada* would still be ours?"

"That's right," replied Laura, stony faced.

"Mum, that's a quarter of a million dollars a year!" shrieked Johnnie.

"So it is," replied Laura.

"But, Mum, I don't understand. I thought you would be ecstatic," said Johnnie.

"There are more important things in life than money," she replied.

"But, Mum…"

They were interrupted by the arrival of the crew. It was Christmas Eve and crowds of excited passengers were beginning to form a queue on the quayside. Laura walked down the gangway and began greeting her guests. They set sail and it didn't take long for the passengers and crew to get into the spirit of Christmas. Before long, they were singing carols, eating mincemeat pies and pulling novelty crackers. Outwardly, Laura gave the impression that she was enjoying the festivities. She joined in with the carol singing and pulled Christmas crackers with the passengers and crew. But inside she felt empty. She had wanted this Christmas to be precious.

A few hours later they were back ashore. She bid her passengers a happy Christmas as they went on their way and the crew began to tidy up *The Morada*. Johnnie gingerly approached Laura and put his arm around her.

"Mum, I'm sorry for being so horrible to you," he whispered. "I have a lot of questions that I need to ask you and maybe now is as good a time as any to ask them. I need to know why Dad left and why you married Nathaniel. And I also need to know why Will has gone away and left us when everything seemed to be going so well."

Laura knew there would come a time when she had to tell Johnnie the truth, and that time had arrived.

"Johnnie, what I am going to tell you might hurt," she replied.

"I don't care, Mum. At least I will know," said Johnnie, softly. "I need to know."

Laura took a deep breath and told him the whole story just as she had told Will not so very long ago.

"What?" he said when she had finished, "He left us with no money at all?"

Laura wrapped her arm around Johnnie and continued. She told him about the gambling debts and the heavy mob who came and took away all of their furniture, and finally she told him about Nathaniel's proposal and how it seemed as if it was her only alternative.

"I had no one else to turn to, Johnnie. I didn't know he was going to be so mean and horrible to us. I just thought a new life would be good for us. I am so, so sorry. You shouldn't have needed to go through any of this," sobbed Laura. "I'm not proud of myself and hope you can forgive me."

Johnnie hugged his mother tightly.

"You should have told me what Dad had done, Mum," replied Johnnie.

"I kept hoping he would contact me and arrange to see you, Johnnie," replied Laura. "I never told you what he did because I didn't want you to hate him. He's still your father."

"Don't you understand, Mum? I blamed you for everything," he said. "You should have told me."

"And as for Nathaniel, I hated myself for taking him up on his offer. I couldn't see any other way out, but I couldn't tell you because I was so ashamed," she said.

"But if you had told me everything, I wouldn't have blamed you or been so horrible to you," said Johnnie.

"I promise, Johnnie, that from now on, I will never keep anything from you again," she said, taking him in her arms.

"What happened between you and Will, Mum?" he asked quietly. "Don't you like him anymore?"

Laura smiled wryly and was preparing her explanation, when a voice from behind her boomed, "Did I 'ear me name bein' mentioned?"

Startled, Laura and Johnnie turned around to find Will standing with his arms open wide, grinning from ear to ear. Johnnie and Laura stared at each other in disbelief, turned and ran into his arms. He pulled them both tightly to his chest.

"You'll never know how good this feels," he said, his voice quivering with emotion.

Laura looked into Will's eyes and placed her hands on his face.

"I'm so sorry, Will," she said, "I just couldn't be the one to…"

"Hush now, it's alright. I know, I know," said Will, interrupting. "And I'm proud and honoured."

"Mum, he's real, Will's real!" exclaimed Johnnie, squeezing Will with all his might. "Feel his arms, he's real again."

"Hold on, lad," laughed Will, "I'll be meetin' me maker soon enough, without you helpin' me on me way."

Johnnie took a step back.

"This means that the curse has been lifted!" exclaimed Johnnie. "But how? It can only be lifted if a woman falls in love with you, Will."

"Aye, that's right lad," replied Will. "Who'd a' thought anyone would honour old Will in this way?"

"But who is it, Will? Did you meet her when you left us?" asked Johnnie.

Laura lowered her head. "It's all my fault, Johnnie. Please don't hate me," she said, dreading Johnnie's response.

Johnnie turned his back on Laura and Will and stood in silence. A few moments later he turned around and faced them again. "You love Will?" he said, his voice trembling.

"Johnnie, I didn't mean to fall …"

"Mum, just answer me," said Johnnie, softly.

Laura closed her eyes. "Yes," she replied.

Johnnie slowly moved towards Laura and Will and snuggled in between them. They huddled together and stood in silence for a while but there was no anxiety or awkwardness, just acceptance.

Eventually, Will let them go and reached into his pocket. He took out two beautiful coloured pebbles and gave one each to Laura and Johnnie.

"It's not much o' a Christmas present," said Will. "But it's from me heart."

"They're beautiful, Will," said Laura.

"Now lad," said Will. "Take your mother's pebble and roll the both of them along the deck."

Johnnie was bewildered by Will's request but took the pebble from Laura and rolled them both along the deck, just as he had requested.

"There you go lad, that's the second part o' yer Christmas present," said Will.

Johnnie looked at Laura, who smiled and shrugged her shoulders.

"What do you mean, Will?" he asked, looking puzzled.

"The Rolling Stones," Will replied, chortling.

Laura and Johnnie shrieked with laughter.

"That's the worst joke ever," said Johnnie, laughing.

All of a sudden Johnnie stopped laughing and covered his face with his hands.

"Mum!" he whispered, "I didn't get Will a present."

Laura stood up and headed down the galley stairs. She returned moments later with a package.

"Happy Christmas, Will," she said smiling.

He stood gazing at the colourful package in his hands. It was the first present he had received in a very long time and it felt so good.

"Aren't you going to open it, then?" said Laura chuckling.

He took off the wrapping paper very gently, enjoying every moment of the anticipation. Inside was a box, which he opened very slowly. There, nestled in white tissue paper, was a sparkling brass plaque. He took it out of the box and read the inscription aloud.

"William Joseph Francis. Captain of *The Morada*." he said, his voice tinged with sadness.

Will stroked the words with his finger. "You two never fail to take me breath away," he said, his eyes welling with tears.

"We'll put it right above the helm so that everyone who boards *The Morada* will see it," said Laura.

Will kissed the top of Laura's head and rubbed Johnnie's hair. "Thank ye both from the bottom o' me heart," he said.

Johnnie lowered his head. He was annoyed with himself because he didn't have a gift for Will.

"I'm sorry, Will; I wanted to give you a present too," he said, unable to look at him.

Will placed his index finger under Johnnie's chin and gently raised his head up so he could look into his eyes. "You gave me the best gift I could ever 'ave asked for, lad," Will replied.

"What do you mean?" asked Johnnie, sullenly.

"The gift of knowin' you, lad," said Will. "You can't buy the most important things in life. You and yer mother taught me that."

Will suddenly slumped forward over the ship's wheel.

"Will!!" exclaimed Laura. "Are you okay?"

"I must be nearin' me time, folks," he replied, trying to straighten himself up. "I feel so weak."

Laura and Johnnie each took an arm and helped Will to sit down. There was silence at the realization that the final part of the curse was coming to pass.

They cuddled into Will and Johnnie began to sob.

"Now, now, lad," said Will, softly. "Stop that hollerin'. You're me first mate, remember."

His eyes filled with tears as he continued, "I'll always be taking a keen interest in you, lad, so you better become a son and a man yer mother can be proud of. Do you hear me?"

Johnnie nodded, unable to speak through his sobbing.

Will took hold of Laura's hand and pulled her gently towards him.

"Thank you, Laura, from the bottom o' me heart," he whispered. "Be happy."

Will's eyes closed and he gently breathed his last breath.

Many a tear was shed, but Laura and Johnnie agreed that from that day forward there would be no place in their lives for bitterness, hate or regret.

✳ ✳ ✳ ✳ ✳

Laura decided to take Mr. D'Angelo up on his offer. *The Morada* toured American harbours and ports for six months of every year but was always in Coral Cove for Christmas. With the revenue from *The Morada,* Laura was able to purchase the big house with the manicured gardens and swimming pool that Will had chosen for them. Pride of place on the marble mantle in the sitting room, she placed the two pebbles.

Johnnie went on to gain an athletics scholarship to the University in Florida, but he still works aboard *The Morada* during the holidays. He wouldn't have it any other way.